Hayati

MY LIFE

Arab American Writing

Hayati

MY LIFE

a novel

miriam cooke

Syracuse University Press

Copyright © 2000 by Syracuse University Press
Syracuse, New York 13244-5160
All Rights Reserved

First Edition 2000
00 01 02 03 04 05   6 5 4 3 2 1

The paper used in this publication meets the minimum requirements of American National Standard for Information Sciences—Permanence of Paper for Printed Library Materials, ANSI Z39.48-1984.∞™

Library of Congress Cataloging-in-Publication Data
Cooke, Miriam.
Hayati, my life : a novel / Miriam Cooke.—1st ed.
p. cm.—(Arab American writing)
ISBN 0-8156-0671-0 (alk. paper)
1. Palestine—Fiction. I. Title. II. Series.
PS3553.O5569 H39 2000
813'.54—dc21   00-032198

Manufactured in the United States of America

For Nawal, Anna, and Rachel

miriam cooke, professor of Arabic literature at Duke University, is author of *The Anatomy of an Egyptian Intellectual: Yahya Haqqi,* (*Choice* Outstanding Academic Book of 1985), *War's Other Voices: Women Writers on the Lebanese Civil War* (1988) and *Women and the War Story* (1997). She is translator and editor of *Good Morning! and Other Stories* (by Yahya Haqqi, and coeditor of *Opening the Gates: A Century of Arab Feminist Writing* (1990), *Gendering War Talk* (1993), and *Blood into Ink: South Asian and Middle Eastern Women Write War* (1994).

Contents

CONTENTS

Chronology

October 1960	Sanaa born
July 1962	**Algerian independence**
May 1964	**Founding of PLO**
June 1967	**June ("Six-Day") War**
June 1967	Assia, Basil, and Afaf move to Kuwait
August 1969	**Israeli air raid on Beirut airport**
December 1976	Samya dies
January 1977	Hasan and Hibba visit Kuwait
May 1980	Aziz and Sanaa marry
August 1980	**Start of Iran-Iraq War**
October 1980	Maryam and Arik marry
May 1982	Jamila born
June 1982	**Israeli invasion of Lebanon**
August 1982	**Expulsion of PLO from Beirut**
December 1982	**Evacuation of PLO from Tripoli**
July 1985	Aziz meets Hibba
December 1987	**Outbreak of Intifada**
December 1987	Arik released
July 1988	**Iraqi "liberation" of Al Faw**
July 1988	**End of Iran-Iraq War**
July 1990	Hibba arrives in Jerusalem
August 2, 1990	**Iraqi invasion of Kuwait**

Hayati

MY LIFE

there was and there was not on the edge of a sea a place called palestine it was a small piece of land just enough for those who lived in it but it was such a nice piece of land that others wanted it it had fruits and flowers and olives and chickens it had beaches and mountains it had villages and towns and cities and it had jerusalem the most beautiful city in the world and jerusalem had mosques and synagogues and churches and everyone wanted jerusalem they wanted her to be theirs and no one else's and god in the sky played solomon and he gave a piece to the muslims and a piece to the jews and a piece to the christians but each wanted jerusalem to be theirs

Assia

August 6, 1990

"Maryam, *hayati*, I love you."

"Mama, please tell me! What's happened to Afaf?"

"They're all right . . . They're going to be all right. I'm trying to work things out and I should be back with you before long."

"Mama! Mama, tell me what's wrong . . ."

"Maryam, if I'm not with you by the end of September, call Layla."

"Mama, be careful. Is there anything I can do?"

"Pray for us."

3

Maryam

October 1960

Mama first told me about my brother when I was twelve. The last class of the first week was history. The teacher announced that the topic this term was the last fifty years in the Middle East. Homework was to ask our parents some questions.

"What kind of questions?" Mama asked.

"Oh, about you. About the war."

"Which war?"

I remember being surprised at how annoyed she had seemed, surprised also she did not know which war the teacher had meant. I hadn't thought much about which war. It had seemed obvious to us kids that our parents would know what the teacher meant.

"Why does she want us to tell her about the war? Isn't she the teacher?" Mama had turned to my grandmother, Sitti, as though she might have the answer.

"Don't worry, child," Sitti had said very quietly. "It's nothing. Just some homework."

I remember being struck by the fact that Sitti had called

4

Mama "child." For a moment I had thought that she was talking to me. Sitti was sitting in her usual corner and embroidering. She turned to me and asked me what the questions were.

"There aren't very many. It won't take a minute. Then I can help with dinner."

If I helped with dinner then I could go and play. Suad and Fedwa's uncle from America had come for a visit and he had brought wonderful things for everyone. The best were the beautiful baby dolls that cried when you turned them over on their tummies. We played with them for hours. I'd never seen anything like them. If Mama could quickly tell me the answers to the questions, there'd be time to play before dinner.

The three of us were sitting in the big living room overlooking the Mount of Olives, and it was just before sunset. This day was like every other day after school when I would sit with them and tell them what had happened that day. The A- in math. The A+ in writing. Ms. Weaver's black hair that had been all black last year, but that this year was suddenly white at the bottom.

"What happened to her? Is she going to die?"

I remember Sitti laughing from her corner.

"Ah, Maryam, *bayati,* always so earnest. No she's not going to die, but she should dye her hair!" The two of them had laughed out loud, and I felt better.

Then, when I'd told them everything, except the way that Fuad chased me around the playground and how afraid I'd been, but also a bit excited because I liked him even though he scared me, I sat down at the dining room table to do my homework.

"OK, so what are the questions?" Mama asked.

"Let me see."

I fished around in my satchel for the list of questions, anxious to do the history homework before Mama changed her mind.

"Here it is. The first question is: when were you born?"

"May 1920."

"Where?"

"Jerusalem."

"When did you marry Baba?"

"May 1945."

"You were 25."

"Good girl," Sitti smiled approvingly, "A in math."

"What are your strongest memories of the war?"

"So, we're back to the war . Which war?"

I didn't know.

"Maryam, I don't know why but I don't like these questions."

"But, Mama, if you don't answer she'll think that I haven't done my homework and I'll get an F."

It had not even occurred to me to ask Baba, even though the teacher had told us to ask both our parents.

"*Hayati*, let's go on with the interview after dinner. Why don't you go over to Fedwa's for an hour. Be sure to be back by 7:30."

After dinner, when Baba had disappeared into Afaf's room as usual, we did the dishes and tidied up the kitchen. Sitti made some white coffee, which Mama brought into the living room. I loved the orange blossom taste and smell of the steaming hot drink.

"Mama, why were you angry with me?"

"Not with you, *bayati*, with the teacher."

"Why?"

"She has no right to go prying into other people's lives."

The evening passed and we did no more of the questions. I didn't dare ask lest she be angry again. Mama went with me to school the next day. When the others handed in their assignments to the history teacher, I waited behind. I had heard that she could be fierce and I dreaded telling her that I could not do the interview. But that day she was not at all fierce. She told me not to worry this time. For the rest of that year I worked extra hard on the history class

Although we did not speak of it again for several months, something had changed. The war had come between us. Uninvited, it had settled into our lives and I knew that there were things that I did not know, that there were questions I was not supposed to ask.

The year passed pretty much uneventfully. Oh, except that Fuad and I kissed once. It was behind the playground after he had chased and caught me. He told me that when we grew up we'd get married.

It was summer. One hot night, I heard Mama and Baba talking in their bedroom. It was odd to be able to hear their voices above the low level hum of their bedtime conversations. Suddenly, I realized that they were quarreling. They tried to keep their voices down but I could hear bits and pieces. The name Usama kept coming up. Gradually, the sounds subsided and I thought I heard Mama crying.

I got out of bed and tiptoed to the door of their room. Silence. Then again the sound of Mama crying. I knocked.

"Mama, are you all right?"

"Yes, *hayati*, go back to bed. Everything's all right."

But the next day she took me into Afaf's room. Baba had just left to buy bread and tomatoes, and Afaf was lying in her bed. Quiet as usual. It was then that she told me her strongest memory from the war.

Assia

June 1946

He had been out on midnight guard duty. It was a still, moonless night and Basil was crouched on his haunches on the brow of a hill above the village. In the distance, hyenas howled. The warm air was silken and fragrant with the smell of wild thyme. Basil found some underbrush that would cover the light of his cigarette. From his back pocket, he took out a leather pouch and unfolded the flap. A whiff of sweet tobacco. He took out the thin white paper and opened it in the palm of his hand. Carefully, he separated and spread out along its length the moist threads of tobacco. When the roll of weed was even from tip to tip, he licked the open edge of paper, folded it over, and ran his thumb down the seam. Lightly moistening his lips, he turned the end in his puckered mouth until it was just right, and then he lit the tip. He inhaled deeply, dragging the smoke down deep. He felt good.

Then, out of that stillness, a shot rang out. Basil froze.

"Where did that come from?" Karim had crawled to where he was stationed.

"Northwest. Where are the others?" Basil whispered urgently.

Karim did not reply. Another shot. And then, a few seconds later, another.

"Shit, I think it's another attack. Where are Umar and Hasanayn?"

Again, Karim said nothing.

The Hagannah had attacked. Basil, Karim, and the brothers, Hasanayn and Umar, had kept up the return fire for as long as they could. But they were only four. The rest of their unit had left that morning, assuming that last week's offensive on the neighboring village meant that it was likely they were going to be spared.

Soon they ran out of the little ammunition they had. The offensive was intensifying. Should they tough it out, or run?

Basil decided that staying was suicidal. He burst into the bungalow he and I had called home for two months. Since the birth of Usama.

I was ready.

I had wrapped a few essentials in one blanket and Usama in another. Basil seized the precious bundle out of my arms and called to me to follow him. We climbed up above the village and through the artillery fire with Hasanayn and Umar in tow. The brothers were inseparable and devoted to Basil, their hero.

"Hey, you two, any idea what's happened to Karim?" Basil called to them over his shoulder.

"He went to his house to save some of his books," Hasanayn yelled back.

"What an idiot! Karim and his precious books." Basil

muttered under his breath, "Marx and God will kill him in the end."

Well, they didn't kill him, but they did take care of his leg.

Others joined us, dark shadows bowed under the weight of what they had been able to sweep together at the last moment.

Suddenly, I don't know why, Basil rushed forward and left me behind. I couldn't keep up but I wasn't really worried because we had agreed to meet at Solomon's Pools. He must have thought that was how he could save the baby and that I could take care of myself.

I remember seeing Basil stumble as he spoke to Usama. Then I lost sight of them.

As suddenly as it had started, the shooting stopped. We had made it through the worst.

I started to run. I needed to see Usama safe and sound in his father's arms. I started to run faster as I felt my panic increase. Where were they? Could they really have gotten so far ahead? Basil must have been running as fast as he could. I ran faster and faster.

Maryam

October 1960

I could feel her panic as she relived the scene. I hoped that the story wouldn't end the way I feared it might. But it did. While Baba was running, the baby had been shot in his arms.

"Ah, Maryam, that baby would have been your brother."

She broke into tears. I waited a bit. The air was slightly stale. Baba said that we should not open the window lest Afaf get sick. I looked over at the bed. Her eyes were wide open.

"So, *hayati*, I hope you understand now why I didn't want to deal with your history teacher's questions?"

I understood about the questions but not about Usama. Why had no one told me about my brother. He would have been fourteen. About Fuad's age. They might have been friends. When I asked Sitti later whether she knew the story she nodded sadly.

"Yes, child, I do"

So, she, too, had known all along and she had not told me. I wondered what other secrets there were and that they were keeping from me. Did they have another life behind my back? If

12

I turned around very, very quickly would I find them doing weird stuff? Was the story really true, or were they making it up?

It turned out that the story was true and lots of people knew about Usama. One day, a week or two later, Mama's friend from the old days, Samira Azzam, came to visit. She had been writing stories about the Resistance and publishing them in papers and magazines all over the Arab world. She was thinking of collecting them into a book. A publisher in Beirut was interested. What did we think of what she had done with the Usama story? Did we mind that she had used it? She would love to include it in the new collection. Of course, she had not used the real names.

"Can I read it?"

Samira looked at Mama, and Mama just shrugged. So she handed me the story. I rushed off to my room to read it in private. As I read it, I realized that it must be true. On paper the story became strange. Not bad strange, just strange, as though it had all happened to someone else. Of course, it had not happened to me, but I felt as though it had. It was no longer only our story, our family tragedy. I couldn't quite tell whether that made it better or worse. I read the last line.

"And then she saw him silhouetted against the early morning gray sky, slightly stooped. Without a word, he handed her the bloody bundle."

That was how Samira ended the story. But the real, the true story went on and on.

Assia

June 1948–April 1949

Two years later, we returned to Jerusalem. I had not seen Maman for four years, and she had not met Basil.

Of course, I had written to her often during those first days of the Resistance. About everything. Literally. My girlfriends had been jealous because they had to keep their activities secret from their parents. Not that the parents did not know. It was just much better for everyone if as little as possible was made of the girls and the guns. That way the fathers did not have to make excuses about absent daughters, and the girls could do what they had to and did not have to lie. I wrote to her about Basil, who at that time was an intelligence officer in the Palestinian resistance. I used to report our conversations about art and music. I knew she would like it that he was so cultured. He was like those people who used to come to our home when Maman had her Tuesday evening salon. That must have been what attracted me to him in the beginning. I remember magic evenings with guests sitting around the living room sipping their drinks and arguing about whether T. S. Eliot was a great poet.

Basil had much to say about the war in Europe and what that might mean for Palestine. He had urged us to attack the British here while they were busy fighting the Germans in Europe.

Then the war in Europe ended. The time seemed right and we married. Just the two of us, a few friends, and the magistrate. I knew that Maman would be disappointed, but I was sure she would understand. We would throw a party for all our friends and relatives when we came to Jerusalem.

But we had to wait a long time. Then, of course, no one was in the mood to celebrate a wedding that had taken place over two years ago.

No, it was not a season for celebrations. The war was over and the British had gone but our real troubles were only just beginning. The Resistance had failed and many were leaving. It was clear that things were going to be different this time for Palestinians. The German, French, Polish, and Romanian immigrants were not like the Turks and the British. These refugees came heavy with horrors, they were not going to send envoys to rule in their place. They had no place of their own. No London. No Istanbul. No Rome. No home.

The new state was not yet a month old, but we all knew that these foreigners were going to be different from those others who had figured in our grandmothers' stories.

When she opened the door on that June morning, she was completely shocked. She went pale and then the tears started to flow. At first, I thought they were tears of joy, but then I realized that she was surprised, shocked perhaps. Yes, I had changed and I knew it.

Her puzzled look sent me back to the moment that the unit photographer had handed me the photos I was going to need for my papers. I had not given a thought to how the loss of Usama had scarred my face. But there it was: white on black in glossy. A haggard, middle-aged woman and I was only twenty-eight.

"Do you like it?" the photographer had asked. "I brushed some of the lines around the eyes."

He had smiled modestly, expecting some little word of praise, some acknowledgment of his artistry. I nodded as I fished around in my purse for the right change so that I would not have to wait for him to break a large note. I counted out the money into his outstretched hand and turned to go.

"Anything wrong? Are you feeling all right, Sitt Assia?"

Basil was wonderful. I felt his old strength return as he supported me, waiting for me or Maman to make the first move. I looked at him and then at her and was suddenly, and in spite of everything, glad that we had come home.

Despite the streak of gray through his thick chocolate hair, he still looked young and handsome. His horn-rimmed spectacles had slipped over the bridge of his nose, and he was wearing a thin-striped white shirt, a camel-colored sleeveless wool vest and black, ever so slightly shiny, pants. He had one arm around me and the other was carrying a battered suitcase.

"I'm honored to meet you, Sitt Samya."

His words broke the spell and I threw my arms around her neck.

"Maman, Maman. Finally, I have been dreaming of this moment."

And then we were both sobbing and laughing. Like all those times when I was a kid and we had quarreled and yelled and ended up in each other's arms, and I would wipe my red, blotchy cheeks and look up at her dear face and loving eyes and feel infinitely comforted. The difference now was that we were both so much older. And the Pond's cream that she slathered on her face at regular intervals throughout the day managed only to produce a polished shine to the deep wrinkles.

Maman gave us three adjoining rooms in the home where I had grown up, a spacious apartment with a view of the Mount of Olives. My old room, Hasan's and the maid's. Nothing much had changed except for the shabbiness and the weight of emptiness. My three brothers had left during my four-year absence, even Hasan, the baby who was not such a baby at 22, had left for Iraq. There seemed to be good opportunities. Maman had been alone in the huge apartment for six months. Small wonder she looked so sad.

Basil was looking for a job with an engineering company, but it was a bad time, and he was still in no shape to take on major responsibilities. Now and again he did some translation work for the U.S. Consulate. Food for a day and then we were back to relying on Maman. We did not talk about Usama. But he was always there, haunting us. The vibrant, brilliant man I married had changed beyond recognition. At night, he tossed and turned and sometimes screamed; his dream world was populated with specters, all of them named Usama. Whereas Usama's death had marked my face, it had branded itself on the soul of his father.

It was a hot summer. In July, the new government ordered the Palestinians in Ramleh and Lydda to leave. We heard reports of refugee camps ringing the borders of the Jewish state. Friends caught inside those borders were escaping with what they could carry and scattering to Lebanon and Jordan. I was in my fifth month and I was getting anxious. How were we going to be able to take care of the baby? I was going to have to do something.

I met with some old friends in the neighborhood. More and more women were working, more and more of them were becoming involved, because their men were disappearing. Any demonstration, however peaceful, was an excuse to crack down and round up men for jail, whether they had been involved in the event or not. And then, of course, many were leaving for the Gulf to find jobs. Hasanayn and Umar had gone to Iraq. When they wrote later from Kuwait, Karim decided to try his luck. He had lost the battle to keep his leg, and without it there was no hope. How was he to survive in a situation where even the able-bodied were unable to find work?

The men were leaving and their women were staying and coping. But I could not do what they were doing. I did not know how to knit or sew or crochet or make lace. I had been brought up to use my head, not my hands, and it seemed too late—or I didn't feel like making a change. So I made a virtue of the necessity. If I was going to have a baby, I was going to have to look after it. So why not look after more than one. That's what we had done in Tulkarem. Whenever a mother had had to go out on a mission, she had to leave her child with someone. Because Basil had been so protective of me, and I was usually at home, I was often the one who ended up with the babies. At the time, I remember, it seemed just as easy, if not easier, to care for three.

So I discussed with Maman the possibility of taking in some of the local children a few mornings a week. To my surprise, she was delighted. The idea of lots of toddlers running around the now-long quiet apartment seemed to revive her sagging spirits and she threw herself into the project.

The meeting went well, even though some of the women were a bit hesitant. What would people think if they left their children with strangers?

"Strangers! Hardly. We've known each other since we were kids."

"What if some stranger wants to leave her child?"

At this point, Maman intervened impatiently.

"That's a different matter altogether. Let's worry about that when the time comes."

Maman's retort had been convincing. If our mothers approved, then others would also.

Basil was less supportive. His gloom deepened. At first, I tried to convince him, but finally I gave up. When I stopped insisting, he stopped objecting. Truce.

Maryam was born in October 1948. The next few months were the happiest I can remember. Happiest, that is, after falling in love with Basil all those lifetimes ago. Everyone said she looked like Basil, and she did with her big brown eyes and long black lashes and thick chocolate hair.

When Maryam was about six weeks old and I felt a bit stronger, we started to get the day care center together. Maman and I busied ourselves rearranging the apartment. We cleared the main part of breakables and valuables. Furniture, knick-knacks, linens, brocades, and old clothes started to pile up in corners everywhere. We talked about tidying up, about putting what we could into boxes and trunks and stashing it all away. But soon we started talking about selling. The new situation was taking its toll on all of us.

One cloudy Sunday afternoon in spring, I went into the living room and surveyed the piles of items that were as familiar to me as the lines in the palm of my hand. It was so hard to think about parting with anything. Everything was precious, but we could not remain fettered to the past by chains of nostalgia.

I spotted in a corner the finely chiseled brass incense burner that had long not been used. It evoked no intense memories. My father got it as a gift from the Azzams in Damascus.

It was not like the dining room furniture with its mother-of-pearl inlay. The stiff, high-backed chairs reminded me of solemn evenings that at the time had been heavy and sad but which now appeared light, filtered as they were through the prism of childhood and present suffering.

Every Tuesday evening, artists and poets gathered in our home and the air filled with smoke and talk. The servants would carry the chairs from the dining room into the living room.

"*Merci*, Fatma. Here, put the chair next to the window. Bring me an ashtray."

No, the censer was different. Beautiful but useless, and remembered as such. It could go. I squeezed through the boxes and furniture.

She was watching me. Before I had had a chance to say anything, Maman nodded approval. She added that there was really no point hanging on to all that clutter.

"There's too much of it, especially since we're no longer entertaining."

I smiled gratefully at her, and rushed out before either of us had a chance to change our minds.

I went to Ahmad's store by the Damascus Gate. Just to get an idea of its value. Ahmad looked at the tall censer and called in his brother.

"Sitt Assia wants to sell it. What d'you think? Twenty dinars?"

"I never said I wanted to sell it. I want to know what it's worth. Just in case I do want to sell it some day. Anyhow, I've heard that the market is great, that they're buying up everything they can lay their hands on."

The brothers looked at each other quickly. Ahmad turned to me.

"Look, just 'cause we know you, twenty-five."

"Come on. You know as well as I that it's worth fifty and you'll probably get eighty for it."

"Tough, that's what you always were. OK. Final price. Thirty dinars and not a fils more. Do you want to ruin us?"

Silence.

"Well, OK. For the sake of your respected mother, Sitt Samya, thirty-five. We'll have to sell it for less."

The way home took me past a carpenter's workshop. He usually put some slightly damaged odds and ends outside the entrance on the sidewalk. This day, I noticed a chest with a chip in the top drawer and no knob on the second. It was no great beauty, but exactly what I was going to need for the toys. I bought it for two dinars. I gave a porter twenty fils to bring it to the house. I bought some baklava from the pastry shop on the corner, some hot falafel from the vendor, six fresh loaves from the bakery.

"I'm home."

"Well? Any luck?"

Maman was embroidering. Her white hair was pulled back in a tight chignon and her face shone in a halo of light from the picture window behind her. She was wearing the long floral housecoat buttoned to the neck that she always wore when she was not expecting visitors.

"I see you don't have the censer." Her tone was curious.

"But I do have lunch and some special treats and the beginnings of a kindergarten," I quipped.

"Congratulations, child, you did the right thing!"

I gave her the remaining thirty-two dinars for safekeeping.

Two weeks later, I was back at Ahmed's. This time, I sold the white linens and silks that had been set aside for my dowry.

Another month, I priced and then sold great-great-grandmother's apple green damask tablecloth.

Quite a bit later, the mother-of-pearl furniture from the dining room. And the matching mirror. And the faded silk prayer rug that a tenant had bought in Qum and then given to Papa when the rent he owed had piled up.

Then the Fatimid turquoise and blue painted bowl.

And finally, the Seljuk cream-colored dish inscribed with burnt sienna letters laced around the edge that the antique dealers had repeatedly wanted to buy and that Maman had always laughingly held on to, saying that it would indeed be a bad day when she sold it.

Afaf
August 6, 1990

Three months after I was born, mother and grandmother opened another center. This one in Bethlehem. Whenever she had a baby, she needed distractions. After Maryam, the Jerusalem kindergarten. After me, Bethlehem. I lay "life-less"—as they insisted on describing me—on Father's lap and he would talk to me, his only real friend, his confidante. How do I know? you ask me. I know because nothing has changed. Whenever we're alone, when she's busy some-where else, he pours his heart out, telling me what he's thinking, what he's feel-ing, why he's doing what he's doing, why she's the way she is, then he blames himself, then her. But it was not always like that. I can still remember, but with a vagueness as though it were someone else's memory, longing for someone else to hold me, to pay me attention, to speak to me as the child, the baby, that I was but was not allowed to be. When they were together they acted as though I were not there. Worse, as though I were deaf. Well, not quite deaf, but, hard of hearing, so that if they lowered their voices that would be sufficient caution against my hearing. But then there were those times when they forgot even that, those times when they became upset, annoyed that I was the way I was. Well, not they, but mother. She never actually said so, just kept worrying about a cure. Father would always come to my defense, go on about what a pretty girl

23

I was and how good! And then mother would say how good Maryam was and how she could not do without her and how a solution had to be found. And then again and again and all over again. I hated Maryam. Well, maybe not hated, but I was jealous of her. Sometimes it would be grandmother and Maryam who would talk. I am sure they were talking about me, and there I was, as though I were a chair, or a rug, or a bug on a bud in a vase in the room with them. They were always sitting together, whispering, sipping tea or lemonade, talking about me. Sometimes, and without asking, they would place a glass in front of me. But I never, never drank from it. One day, when I was old enough to have my own memories, but too young to know when that was, I heard grandmother tell Maryam that children like me should be received as a blessing. A blessing? Maryam had asked. Grandmother answered the question with a question. Was not blindness a sign of sure sight? And then she went on to describe how for a while I had brought "light back to your father's eyes and cheeks." Light in his cheeks! Now, that was quite something! After saying this, or something like it, she paused meaningfully. "He sat by her crib for hours as though waiting for her to awake and to cry and to need to be held. But she neither wakened nor slept. She just lay there frozen, eyes wide, staring at the ceiling." Ugh! "He sat in that room for hours on end with his back slightly turned to the still child. For weeks, he stayed indoors. The children continued to come to the apartment. They rushed up and down in the next room, laughing, screaming, crying, while the two of them stayed still." Grandmother went to the storeroom for some turquoise thread to complete the peacock's tail. That was the one thing I really liked about her. Those rich bird tapestries. "For the first time since your mother opened the center seven years ago, he did not escape at dawn. He stayed by Afaf's side without moving. Whenever your mother popped her head around the door, he would motion her away, as though to say it's all under control. From time to long time, he would turn to the baby, pick her up, and gingerly place the rubber nipple in her mouth, and she would duti-

fully suck. Basil held the warm little bundle to his heart." I remember that. Yes, he at least had tried. Once I heard mother tell grandmother how surprised she had been when Father had taken such an interest in me. He had scarcely noticed Maryam's birth. But with me, it was different. And then the two of them would reminisce about the moment I was born. Had I been the vase of the bud in the room, they would have paid me more mind. Apparently, Father was sitting in the waiting room with grandmother when the doctor entered, looking grim by all accounts. It was a girl, he had announced, and there was something wrong. Father had become very agitated and rushed out of the waiting room and into the ward, even though men were not supposed to be there. Then, mother filled in, he could not be persuaded to go, but insisted on holding me. At first, she was happy to see him once again alert and caring. But something was not quite right. He was holding me too tight. He always held me too tight. When the nurse came to hand me back to mother, Father seems to have tightened his grip. He could feed me, take care of me, he told the nurse. She looked at him in alarm and then at mother. Grandmother saved the day, or so she said, by arriving in the nick of time and saying: "Well, how are things? Why, Basil, look at you! I thought you didn't know how to hold a baby!" That must have gone down well with Father! She seems to have thought that her cheery voice lightened the heaviness in the room, and the nurse shuffled out, muttering under her breath. Maryam laughed. And I remember being so angry. What was so funny! Were they laughing at Father or at me? I was sure they were laughing at me and I was angry even though they never knew. And surely did not care. From then on, mother claimed she was too exhausted to fight, to insist that she wanted to hold me. So I was abandoned to Father's obsessive care and possessive silence. I grew accustomed to his fierce clamming up whenever anyone entered the room. I never became used to the dreadful echoing loneliness. When Father was not with me, he was at Ali's Cafe. When I was a little older but still in that time before memory, he would leave me each morning as soon as the kids came. He slipped out of the back door and then down the fire escape past the garbage cans and then out into the street. Mother complained that Father was often Ali's first customer of the day. He would buy the newspaper, order his coffee, and then settle into his corner. When he was sure the children had left, he'd sneak back to resume his vigil. I got to know people through the stories he told me about them. About Hasanayn and Umar who went to Iraq. About Karim, who had joined them. About Usama . . . When I was born, Usama would have been nine years old. I would have had a big brother. We could have talked. He would have been my protector and friend and he would have understood me. Yes, we would have spoken to each other. And because he would have been alive, there would have been no need for Maryam to be born. Just the two of us. Usama would have protected me against everyone. He would have made sure Father did not lock me away and talk at me for hours and hours without expecting or waiting for a reply.

Assia

January 1961

It was when Afaf was about five that I began to realize that my problems with Basil were not going to go away. I also knew that we had to do something about Afaf. But how and when? I was always so busy, checking on the safe arrival of some item or other, working out a problem at the Bethlehem center. Maman had been encouraging in the beginning, but she was becoming frail. The excitement at the thought of the kids in the house had been dispelled by their exhausting reality. She was aging under my eyes and becoming frustrated with her growing weakness. Most discouraging and difficult was Basil.

"No," I told him, "I can't leave it to Fatima."

"So what's the point of calling her 'Director,' if she doesn't know how to direct the center?"

"Of course, she does, but she's too close to Nadya, Salma's mom."

"What in the hell does that have to do with anything?!"

"Basil, are we going to have to go through the same stuff again and again? Will you never understand how hard it is for

these women to go out and work in the center? I wish I didn't
have to go each time there's a hitch, but I do. So that's it."

"I still don't understand what's the matter with Nadya."

His peevish tone was beginning to rankle.

"Too bad!"

I shrugged in annoyance and put on my jacket. But Basil was
not giving up.

"So you're just going to go off for a couple of days and
you're not going to tell us why! What about Maryam? She's
going to think that her grandmother is her mother. And I sup-
pose I have to look after the brats in the morning!"

Wow, if he wanted my attention, he had it. I exploded.

"Since when have I ever asked you to do anything with the
children? You're a mess. Useless. You can't keep a job. You can't
help around the house because you're always too bloody sad,
too fucking sorry for yourself. What about me? Was Usama your
son only? And who was it that was holding him when he was
shot?"

I felt sick with pain as I picked open the wound neither of us
had dared touch. But there it was. In a moment of rage, I had
spoken the unspeakable. Basil was white. I longed to go over to
him and to hold him and have him hold me. But I didn't. The
habit of distance persisted despite the shock. I went on numbly
as though I had not said what I had just said.

"Maman has the situation perfectly in hand." I was not
convincing.

A small pause.

"Anyhow, I'll probably be able to come right back tonight. I
don't understand the fuss."

I was exhausted, and my anger evaporated. For a moment, I had seen the handsome, brilliant engineer I had fallen in love with all those centuries ago. But the mention of Usama had dropped the mask back down.

"Save me some soup if I'm not back in time for dinner."

I caught the first bus to Bethlehem.

Fatima explained what happened. Salma hadn't shown up Thursday and hadn't let her know. She'd had to fill in. But as soon as the last kid had been picked up, she'd gone to Salma's. To her amazement, Salma's mother, Nadya, answered the door and insulted her. Fatima and Nadya were childhood friends and they always told each other everything. But that Thursday, Nadya insulted her. She said that Fatima was trying to dishonor her, trying to turn her daughter into a prostitute. Nothing Fatima could say would calm her down. In fact, Nadya had been so angry that she started to talk with the mothers of the other women working at the center. She told them that their daughters were not taking care of children but that the center was some kind of a front and that their daughters were really going there to meet men. She told them that Fatima was arranging these meetings, that she was probably being paid. That the center was probably a brothel.

This was worse than usual, I thought as I made my way to Nadya's house. Fatima and Nadya had known each other forever. Things had to be pretty bad if Sitt Nadya was so upset. Wasn't she the one who had made a special trip to Jerusalem, just before Suez, to beg me to help them open another center in Bethlehem? Afaf was only eight months old, and it seemed like the last thing I should be doing. Nadya, however, had spent time here at the center when she was in town. She loved the bustle of the kids playing and screaming, and she would give me ideas, suggest activities for the older children. So I decided that if the women agreed to run it, I could probably help without too much effort. Nadya was delighted and she suggested that because Fatima had some business experience she should be the director. Was this troublemaker the same Nadya who had assured me that there would be no problems? What on earth could have happened to make her change so drastically?

The reception I got was ice cold, only just polite. No, she would not allow Salma to go back to the center. How could she when everyone was talking?

"Sitt Nadya, since when do we care that people are talking? Let them! You know perfectly well what we're doing. If we were to stop the meetings, there'd be no hope at all. We might as well just get jobs in Israel. Why not take out Israeli citizenship? How about it? Sound OK to you?"

As usual, I was getting annoyed, frustrated that it was still so hard to hold on to people I had thought were with me.

On the bus back, I mulled over the happenings of the day. It had turned out to be quite a success. Convincing Nadya to change might be a small thing, but it was a kind of a victory.

"Basil, *ya habibi*, the soup's delicious! Thanks for waiting up. I was dying to tell you all about it."

"Sitt Nadya was always a good sort. I guess that's why I was so insistent . . ."

He had been warming some bread and at that point he looked at me a bit mischievously.

"That's why I was such a bore this morning. I guess."

He came over to the table. After setting down the bread, he leaned toward me and kissed me softly on the lips.

"I love you, darling."

"I love you, too."

It sounded mechanical, but because we so rarely exchanged tendernesses, it was not. And I did love him. I still do, especially when he is just a little less sad.

"I couldn't believe that you had to go all that way to talk with Nadya of all people."

"Who knows how long it will last. If it's not her, next time, it might be her neighbor or her sister or even Salma herself. The mayor's committed, but the women are not. At least not all of them, and the minute someone comes up with some conspiracy theory or other, everyone's in a panic. Brothel. Military head-quarters. Contraband. Whatever will they dream up next? Who would have ever guessed that the men would be more support-ive than the women. These men who could not imagine their wives and daughters working outside the four walls of their houses are actually approaching us and offering to help with the centers."

Basil looked ashamed and I felt guilty again.

Maryam

May 1964, June 1967

The first time Afaf showed me a drawing, she was eight and I fifteen. It was then that I realized that she understood perfectly what was going on around her. Afaf had gone off, as usual, after breakfast when the children started to turn up and Baba had gone to the cafe. Mama didn't worry anymore because Afaf had been doing this ever since she could walk. The first time, Mama had rushed off in a panic, calling out her name between sobs. But Afaf had not gone far. She never went far. She always went to the same place, the water tower. She would sit next to it, deep in concentration, constructing an image. At first, she used scrap paper she'd picked up off the streets and a blunt pencil the grocer let her have. When Mama caught her the first time, she punished her because she thought she'd stolen the pencil. Afaf looked at her coldly. I never saw Afaf cry, certainly never heard her. But then she went up to her bed and climbed under the covers. All in complete silence. She stayed there like a stone for two days. She ate nothing, drank nothing. Finally, Mama gave in and told her that it was OK, that she could go to the water tower to

32

draw. I think the grocer must have told her about the pencil. After that no one thought much about Afaf's disappearances. Even I forgot. Actually, I'd always been a bit jealous. She was so pretty, so fragile. I wanted her to love me. Sometimes I convinced myself that she really could speak and that she was just trying to annoy us by saying nothing.

I wanted her to love me, to need me. I wanted her to put her arms around my neck. Once, I tried to scare her so that she would want to be protected and then she would put her arms around my neck. So I hid and when she came looking for me, I jumped out and shouted Boo! I did scare her. But she didn't put her arms around my neck. Anyway, Baba was so obsessed with her that I decided not to love her.

I wouldn't let her play with my friends. Whenever she hung around the room where we were playing with my dolls, the ones Baba had bought for me before she was born, I just told her to go away. I was really mean. I'll never forget my eleventh birthday. I had my school friends over and we were all playing and having fun, when Afaf showed up. I knew it was going to happen, so I was prepared.

"Go away, you're too little."

I knew she didn't like it when I told her she was too little to play with me and my friends. But this time, she didn't go away as usual, looking hurt. This time, she just stayed there, glued to the spot. I pushed her a bit. Afaf was only three and a half, but she was strong. She stood there in the middle of the room, in the middle of my friends.

"What's wrong with her?"

"Why doesn't she do what you tell her?"

And then the big question.

"Why doesn't she ever say anything?"

They didn't know. They'd seen her before, but she always did what I'd asked her to do. I didn't tell anyone because I was ashamed. I mean, it was weird having a baby sister who couldn't speak. It was weird enough having a mother who was out all the time. I didn't need to have people know that I had a mute sister. Maybe they'd think I was weird, too, and wouldn't want to play with me, even though Fedwa and I were the only ones I knew who had dolls. Not that the boys were interested in the dolls. They were just there for the party.

But then it happened. The full catastrophe! Maryam's great humiliation! As the kids were standing there looking at her, Afaf had a temper tantrum. She just threw herself on the floor and kicked and screamed odd little stifled screams. I was thunderstruck. I had never seen her do anything like it . . . I was not at all prepared . . . So I thought that the best thing would be to try and calm her down . . . Anything, just as long as I could get rid of her, and pretend that nothing had happened. So, I knelt next to her and started to pat her on the back. I kept stroking her and calling her name. Finally, she seemed to have gotten over the worst, and I felt her relax. I pushed her a bit to get her to turn on her back and sit up. Suddenly, she lifted her leg and kicked me in the face, as her foot came down it caught the front of my dress and ripped the shoestring straps that held it in place. I couldn't believe it . . . There I was. Naked in front of my friends, the little boys staring at my acorn breasts!

Then, I remember nothing significant until that evening in 1964, when we turned on the radio and heard the announcement of the Arab ministers gathered in East Jerusalem. Everyone had been talking about it, but no one dared believe it. At last, the Palestinians had an official body—the PLO—to represent them in their struggle against Israel. The neighbors came over with champagne. And even though I was only fifteen, I was allowed to take a sip. Wow, what a party we had. But we forgot Afaf. She sat in her corner as usual and we clean forgot. Next day, she came into my room carrying a large satchel. She was agitated. She sat on the floor and opened the satchel. It was full, packed with drawings and paintings.

"Where did you get these?"

Afaf tossed her head impatiently and pointed to her chest.

"When did you do them?"

For the first time I was talking to her as though she could understand and respond. Ignoring my question, she started to lay them out on the floor. There were crayon drawings, watercolors, some collages. She carefully unfolded a collage. It was huge—about four feet by six! Then she laid it on top of the others.

Up in the left-hand corner I saw a tent suspended as though from heavenly ropes. Then that tent fused with another that hung suspended from the top of the composition.

At the center of that top tent was an eye, a large weeping eye. There were eyes . . . everywhere. In the clouds above the tents, in the ground below them. And all the eyes were weeping. The ground that was painted as though vertical was littered with bodies. With corpses. All strangely swollen. Wounds with blood pouring out of them and into the thirsty earth. There was a Palestinian flag flying above the side tent. When I asked Afaf what it all meant, she shrugged. But her agitation had increased.

I started to rummage through the smaller drawings and saw that they were all of children. Some of them were throwing stones. They were alone, sometimes throwing at something outside the frame of Afaf's troubled vision. Mostly they were in groups. Sometimes as many as eight. Boys and girls together.

Years passed. Then, one day in the summer of 1967, just after that terrible war, Mama announced that the three of them were going to Kuwait to get treatment for Afaf. They'd be back for Christmas.

"You'll stay with Sitti. Think how much fun you'll have with her. She spoils you rotten!" Mama pinched my cheeks. "We'll be back soon. You'll see."

She was upbeat, trying to make it sound as though they were off on a holiday and would be back in two weeks. I felt that I'd been right all along and that she did prefer Afaf, after all. Maybe she'd just pretended to love me and ignore Afaf. Maybe it was like it had been with the Usama story, and they were saying things behind my back. I wrote hateful things about both of them in my diary.

Mama went on and on about how lucky I was to be well and smart and top of my class, and how Afaf needed help. Good, I thought, let them go, and the whining will stop. Maybe they'll learn that Afaf's really fine, she's not sick. Look at her paintings and you'll see . . . But they knew nothing because they'd never looked at them. She was not quite human for them. As Sitti would say, "one of God's blessed."

Afaf
August 6, 1990

Here we are again. Back at square one. Yet not back, somehow different. We are not who we were. This is not the place we went to when we first arrived. They knew what they were doing when they came here. It was not random. It was the museum whose belly yesterday belched fire and smoke and stank like a papermill. It was the Emir's palace. It was the hotels on the Gulf shore. It was the homes of the rich and oblivious and the homes of those who wanted to be like them. When I was eleven, Usama would have been twenty-one. He would have been a fidai and he would certainly have been a leader. He would have fought and made sure that we won. But Usama died forty-four years ago and so we lost the wars of 1956 and of 1967 and our beautiful city was split. And so was our family. Grandmother said she was staying. Like great-aunt Najwa when Haifa was taken in '48, she decided to stay. I thought that if grandmother stayed, whatever that meant, we were all staying. But I was wrong. Night after night, in grandmother's room, mother talked with Father and Maryam and grandmother about what they should do. Sometimes their voices rose in anger. And although it was was hard to hear from my room, I did make out something about Maryam, about whom she did not have to worry. Year after year, she had come out top in her class. Her teachers thought she should study abroad. But as for Afaf . . . Right. That was me. They were talking about me and the tone immediately changed, became querulous. What was the big deal? I didn't bother them. So what if I didn't speak? Yet they went on and on about what would happen to "this poor girl born with the bomb. Eleven years old and never uttered a word." Was this a crime!? The doctors told mother that I was still in shock. It was during Suez. There were bombs dropping. One dropped near our home. The explosion had shattered the windows and her placenta. The baby, me, arrived a month early without a sound. I scarcely cried. You'd have thought they'd be pleased. The first time I remember mother ever looking at me as though I was capable of understanding was when I was about seven. She came into my room one afternoon after the children had gone and before Father came home from Ali's. She walked straight toward me. There was something frightening about the way she was looking at me and I ran away and hid in a corner, my face in my hands against the wall. I was not prepared for the gentleness in her voice. "Afaf, my heart, come here. Let's go. Mummy wants you to get better. Let's go see Sitt Khairiya." This was the first time I had heard the name. It was also the first time mother had spoken quite like this. I wanted to tell her I was happy she had come to see me, to speak to me, to take me out. But I could not. It was like now, as though everything had gone dead inside me, black outside me, and from somewhere far away I herd a terrible howling. Who could that be? What a dreadful pain to produce such a horrible sound! Several days later, while I was still in bed in the dark, velvet-hung room, mother returned. It was the first time since she had talked to me about Sitt Khairiya. Father, of course, was out. She had insisted that I be kept in my room until I got better, and that, no, there should be no light. She tiptoed into the room followed by a fat woman in black who was muttering something. "Here she is, Sitt Khairiya. She's been quiet for the past three days. But I'm afraid she might have another attack." "Should we talk so loud?" "Don't worry, the girl understands nothing." Yet they did start to whisper and

I could not make out what it was that they were saying. Then the fat woman came to my bedside. She held my hand and put something cold and wet on my forehead, all the while mumbling away. Then she started to fiddle with some paper. I opened my eyes the tiniest crack to watch what she was doing. I saw her write on a scrap of paper and then put it into a bowl of water. After swirling the paper around, she made me drink that dirty water, and mother did not stop her. She wrapped the wet, washed paper into a piece of leather, which she carefully tied into a little bag. Then she wound a leather string around the top of the bag and hung this necklace around my neck. Every day for what seemed like forever after that, I had to drink a thick, bitter potion before going to bed. And I only drank it because Father assured me, after mother had assured him, that it was good for me. But all that it did was to give me a rash and constipation. So the doctor had to come and give me some medicine to cure me from the medicine. "Will you not give up, Assia? The girl was fine and now she's sick and ugly and unhappy." "How can you say she's unhappy when no one can tell if she's ever happy? She's not crying. She looks about the same as ever. In fact, a bit better. I could have sworn that she was trying to say something yesterday. I passed by her room and I heard a sound that could have been 'Mummy.'" Well, it was not "Mummy," mother! The discussions and arguments about whether or not I was sick continued but I never did see Sitt Khairiya again. Mother, it seemed, was determined to leave. Had it not been for Afaf, I heard her once explain with a little apology stuck halfway down her throat, she would have stayed. Lucky for her she had me, I had thought, otherwise how could she do what she wanted to do and not feel totally and completely guilty. "This is no place for the already helpless." Echoes from Karim. "We've got to go to Kuwait." You might well ask why Kuwait? Well, it happened like this. A year earlier, Cousin Layla from Kuwait came to visit. She was very elegant. All brown and beige and lots of gold and perfect hair swaying to the shoulders. I could not take my eyes off her. Layla was perfect.

Her husband was a doctor, she told us proudly, and he would certainly be able to help me. Help me do what? I had wondered. Father told her that I was fine. And the women all looked at each other meaningfully and then pretended that they had not looked. She had added breezily that they would have to bring me to Kuwait. "Why's that?" "Obviously, Akram cannot come back." Mother looked at Layla questioningly. "He was in the Resistance, you know. And his family's from Jaffa. He's on a list." There had been pride in her voice when she spoke the last words. So we had no choice. Because Father and I did not count for much in these discussions, it was finally decided that we should go. Maryam was to stay with grandmother. It was not easy. To get to Kuwait, mother had to contact an agent, who arranged for her, Father, and me to cross the desert. Wherever we went, mother would arrange the next step. She would leave Father and me somewhere to wait. Then, after a long or short while, she would return and we would be briefly hectic, bustling on and off buses or trucks. It was a long, terrible trip. But it was the first time the three of us had been together, just us, without Maryam and grandmother, and I was glad we had left. Layla had not been so enthusiastic when she found the three of us on her marble doorstep. She pulled us in off the threshold, afraid the neighbors might see us. They lived in a large square house in Salmiya, the only district in the whole of Kuwait City that had allowed non-Kuwaitis to move in next to Kuwaitis. But if they wanted to retain the privilege, they had better not have riffraff prowling at their doors. She called Fatouma and told her to get us clean. She would get us some fresh clothes . . . Mother and Father were so exhausted they did not react to the unexpectedly chilly reception. Leaving smudges on the white marble hall floor, we trudged behind Fatouma. Through the kitchen and down the back staircase. There we found ourselves in a much darker, tighter, hotter space. Fatouma, now more intimate, put her arm around me and led me to the end of the corridor. She said nothing and seemed not to expect anything from me. I liked her. She showed us the bathroom, a simple room six feet by six. In one corner was the squat toilet and in the other was a drain in the floor under an overhanging pipe. The sweet smell of sandalwood had not found its way down here. While Father allowed the cold water to pour out on his head, mother and Fatouma undressed me. All that could be heard was the splashing of the shower on the concrete floor. After a few minutes, the water stopped and we heard him humming. We looked at each other in surprise, and smiled. It was as though we had known each other for a long time. An hour later, the four of us trooped upstairs, freshly bathed and strangely clothed. Fatouma remained at a slight distance, once again the servant. Layla floated down the marble stairs into the hall, where we stood clinging to each other. She was wearing a white silk caftan embroidered with white around the neck and sleeves. She had recovered her composure. "Please, come in." She waved us into a beautiful room hung in cream-colored raw silk with burgundy red velvet reclining benches lining the walls. At regular intervals stood small octagonal tables, each with a blue glass bowl filled with pastel-colored, sugar-coated almonds. "Please. Make yourselves comfortable. Help yourselves. What can I get you? Coffee? Tea? Or maybe something cold? What would Afaf like?" The latter remark was addressed to mother, whom Layla had chosen to be my interpreter. When no one replied, Layla whispered something to Fatouma who disappeared. She turned back to us. "Oh dear! I just wish I'd known you were coming." I knew that mother had written, so why did she say this? "I would have liked you to stay with us. At least, in the beginning. But, you see, we're about to leave for Paris. It's just too hot here in the summer. Nobody stays in this hellish heat." Silence. Layla continued nervously. "Unfortunately, we can't even entertain you tonight because we've been invited to the hospital director's grande soirée." She lingered on the French words a bit. The mention of the soirée had perked her up. "It is the social event of the year. The last get-together before everyone's off to their summer place." Curious, how she emphasized certain words. I had a feeling she was not talking to us, but to a camera *inside her head. Layla paused uncertainly, as though she had suddenly heard herself. Tentatively, she suggested. "Of course, I could turn it down." Her tone was not encouraging, and we looked at her blankly. Layla chose to take our silence to mean that we would not expect such a sacrifice. She added, as though this was the clinching argument, "And I've just bought a dress for the party." Layla could not control a little involuntary smile of pleasure at the thought of the dress. Then, again earnest and serious, she said, "Obviously, you'll spend tonight here. Fatouma will make something delicious." She smiled at me the way you smile at an idiot, one of God's blessed, and I remembered what grandmother had told Maryam. "So what are your plans?" Father and mother exchanged startled looks. They had no plans. Their plan had been to get to Kuwait. So here we were. They had not planned beyond that plan. They had thought that Layla would take care of the rest. After a heavy silence, Layla stood up and announced that she had to call her husband. She would be right back. We should help ourselves. While she was gone, we said nothing. The fatigue of the journey seemed suddenly nothing in comparison with the weight of disappointment. I pulled my legs up under me and curled into the cushioned corner made by the meeting of the banquettes. "Well, I spoke with Akram. He's such a darling. He told me not to worry and that Suha would take care of everything." Worry? Layla did not seem to be worrying too much. I did not like the way she spoke, the little scattered emphases that punctuated her sentences. She was rattling on and on about how wonderful Akram's secretary was and how she would find us whatever we needed: a place to live, a job, and, yes, an appointment with Akram's colleague, the speech therapist. We stayed for a couple of nights and then we moved out. Suha was as good as Layla said she was. After arranging and paying for a week in a modest hotel, she found us an apartment in Hawalli. Everyone in our building was Palestinian. The neighbors were welcoming and the new home was quite comfortable. Mother took the first job she was offered. Our life acquired a rhythm. For mother, there* was the daily shuttle between the new home and the palace of the third wife of the Emir's second cousin, where she was tutoring the girls in mathematics. She maintained the obsessive management of scarce resources. For Father, things did not change much. Sometimes he worked, sometimes not. I painted. A few years later, I got a job teaching art at a small school.

Assia

December 25, 1969

Dearest Maman and Maryam,

Merry Christmas. We miss you. I can scarcely believe that we've been gone over two years. How are you both? Did you go to Bethlehem for Midnight Mass?

We are fine and getting used to things here. Yesterday, we had a modest celebration. I actually found some Christmas lights to hang around the doors and on a little artificial tree that Sitt Zulaykha gave us. They don't celebrate Christmas, but last December her husband had had to entertain some English businessmen and they had ordered the tree from a shop in London called Harrods. Apparently, the party had been a terrible failure. She insisted that I take the tree because they did not need it. So things got quite festive here. She also gave us some gifts, including some clothes for Afaf. The dresses were too big, but they would fit you, Maryam. Some of the dresses are really gorgeous.

We've seen Dr. Farwan, but he did not say much. He ran a few tests and we've not heard the results. He told us to make another appointment, but he is so busy and hardly ever in town. Layla keeps telling me that he is the best and that he will certainly know what to do.

We've just had a little hike in the rent which is why the check is a bit smaller. I'm so sorry and hope that it won't be too much of a problem.

How is the university, Maryam?

The best news is that Baba has just been offered a job in an engineering company run by Layla's father-in-law.

Soon we'll all be together again. I love you both.

> Your loving daughter and mother,
>
> Assia

I blotted my name carefully and then glanced at the corner. Then out of the window at the blank wall. I shivered for the end of another year and for my loneliness and longing for home. Would Basil finally meet with Tariq? Layla had made it all sound so easy.

"My father-in-law is in with the sheikhs. They've invested in his company, and he is going to employ Palestinians only, if possible. Obviously, first preference will go to the family."

At a sign of modest demurral on my part, Layla had insisted.

"Really, Assia! You know you're family!"

Well, family, no family, it seemed there were other cousins ahead of Basil. The tomorrow of the interview was always the day after tomorrow, and as time crawled by, Basil grew angry and bitter. I knew it was hard for him to have to go on depending on my income from tutoring what he called the "spoiled brats."

Poor boy! But what could I do? How to deal with his tantrums? What an odd year this has been. The first man has landed on the moon. The Israelis attacked the Lebanese airport.

Afaf had her first period. She had another of her blackout attacks when she saw the blood. But then she got better. She's not a helpless child any longer, but a woman, a startlingly beautiful woman. Basil was annoyed when I told him about her period. Who knows why, but I guess that he must have realized she could no longer be his baby, at least not the way he wanted.

I wonder what Hasan is doing? He must be living not too far from here. Baghdad? And Hibba. It would be nice to see them. Maybe I can make some inquiries.

Maryam

December 9, 1976

Darlings,

Sitti died three hours ago, at 9 P.M. For three days she was whispering urgently, fiercely. I don't know what she was trying to say. I fear she did not die in peace. More than ever I wish we could be together.

Maryam.

I sat by Sitti's bed, my pink right hand lightly enfolding the small, shriveled yellow gray fingers. The bedside lamp gave out a weak glow that drew the walls closer to the bed.

I eased my chair even closer with my left hand, seeking companionship in this hollow darkness. Time seemed to have stopped. I only knew it had not because of the touch of the fingers under my unmoving hand. For the first time, I felt a little afraid. I had asked the people who had come to pay their condolences to wait in the hall for a bit. I needed to be alone with Sitti for one last time. I felt absolutely and completely alone except for the shadows playing on the walls. They seemed alive, spectators watching me. Slowly, I withdrew my hand and raised myself slightly out of the chair. I leaned over the body that was taking up less and less space on the bed. I felt a sudden surge of tenderness and loss. I wanted to hold on to this carnal memory, to refuse its utter emptiness. For twelve years, we had been alone together, seen each other every single day. There was no one on earth with whom I had known such closeness.

The last month I had moved her to a place where they could take better care of her than I could. I had visited her every day, sometimes twice. Usually, just around mealtime so that I could help her. I had felt closer than ever to her. Yet, when I looked at this familiar face, the smoothed out, stretched out peacefulness of the features filled me with dread.

I placed my lips on the yellow forehead. It was ice cold. The finality of this departure was marked by the presence of an empty body and for the first time I understood in a way beyond words what was soul, a fullness of sadness and joy, of anger and hope, of bitterness and sweetness. And no matter how hard life had been, it was so much more than this.

"Sitti, why did you have to die? You were supposed to live forever."

The shadows frowned disapprovingly, and I felt self-conscious, surprised at the sound of my own voice in that silent chamber.

I have often thought back on that moment and how my grief had been disturbed by that sense of theater. Sometimes, the memory is so vivid that it is as though Sitti has come back, only to die again. And then, all over again I feel that wrench, that terrible certainty that I'll never see her again. Never again be able to surprise her with a little something that became so special when she acknowledged it so gratefully.

The women started to file in past the bed. Some looked at the body stretched out in stony repose. Those were the curious. Some walked with their eyes averted, fixed on some spot ahead of them, not daring to look at the face of death. Those were the fearful. For them, Sitti was no longer, and what remained there in that chamber was the macabre mask placed over the dread that dwelt in their souls, the certainty that this was their destiny also.

Then came the men and the pallbearers and the commotion of the *levée du corps*. They carried the stretcher out of the room and headed to the stairs. When I rushed forward to touch her just one last time, I felt hands grab my arms from behind. The women were holding me back as their wailing rose.

"I want to be with her when they put her in the ground."

The wailing increased to a high pitch. I had said the ritualistically correct words, so no one paid me any attention. But I meant them. I'd seen the scene several times when I had attended others' funerals and I had always wondered about the women. How could they let themselves be so easily restrained if they really felt what they seemed to be feeling.

Strangers would be with her in this final moment, and I was screaming at the injustice. At the stupidity of it all. But no one paid me any attention, and I stayed with the women.

The last head disappeared around a turn in the stairs. I ran to the window and watched the procession follow the flat stretcher covered in white linen down the street. Sitti was so small she scarcely disturbed the white flatness.

She was gone and I was left with these women and their whispered gossipings and the incessant flow of black coffee.

Hibba

August 3, 1990

I knew all about Maryam, so it was odd that she knew so little about me. I had to start from scratch. Mother. The Women's Teacher Training College at Basra. Graduated summa in May 1980. The work at an advertising agency in downtown Baghdad.

I was the only woman at Nur Advertising. Twelve men and me fresh out of school. After each man had tried his luck and been rebuffed, word got around that there was something wrong with me. I might be a . . . ! Lots of winks and nods and innuendos made words superfluous. I couldn't care less, as long as I could work. Wasn't this the way professional women were always treated?

At least, that was how things usually worked out in the Egyptian novels and stories I read in high school. Yusuf Idris and Naguib Mahfouz had warned me again and again about what happened to women who thought that they could walk into a man's world. Like Cairo, like Baghdad.

But I was doing what I loved doing. And . . . I was being

50

paid to do it! Even as a child, I loved to spend hours doodling on any scrap of paper I could lay my hands on.

One day, my boss asked me to make a sketch for a soap ad. I penciled a woman's face and then applied the paint of the skin so tight, so pure and translucent that it seemed separate from the bones and muscles that then began to fill in underneath.

When he looked over my shoulder, he exclaimed out loud.

"You know how much I admire your drawing, Ms. Lughod. But this is not the kind of thing that we do here. We have to make the product, whatever it is, appealing. This face is frightening, it looks as though the soap had abraded the skin down to the bone. We want beauty, health, and customer appeal. We want people to consume what we advertise without thinking, as though they had finally found what they had been looking for all their lives."

He did not even crack a smile. I knew better than to react, except with a nod of understanding.

"I see. I'll do my best."

I was a quick learner. Soon my drawings were the ones that were the most frequently chosen. Throughout the war, I held my job. In fact, I became known for my precise, accurate portrayals of whatever it was that had to be marketed. Sometimes the corporations would not make it quite clear what exactly it was they were trying to sell, and I would question the representative until I could see not so much the product as what its advocacy was supposed to achieve. Oddly enough, for me at least, life seemed to continue as normal while Saddam was waging his war, his legendary Qadisiya, only a few hundred miles from us.

Then an insecticide company was taken on as a new client.

The director was all excited because this was going to be one of our biggest jobs yet. The company had just made a revolutionary discovery and they were mounting a massive campaign, claiming that its product could kill not only the usual household creepie crawlies, but that it could also zap larger, stronger varieties, like scorpions and snakes.

Quite some claim. As I sat down to produce the sketch, I realized that I would have to do something different this time. It was my chance to do what I liked to do best, to get inside the object and work with it organically. How could I make the image most effective? What if I were to draw the insect's body but with a human head? Yes, that would do it. Then I could show the pain and how utterly effective the poison was.

"What's going on? What's this?"

My boss, as usual, had sidled up without my noticing so as to watch me. He pointed at the beginnings of an outline of an insect, an insect with an almost human, definitely suffering face.

"My drawing for the insecticide people."

"You've got to get rid of that human head!"

"Why? I thought it would be particularly effective to show the pain, and the utter finality of the poison. As you yourself once told me, it's very important for the customer to see what it is that the product is going to do."

"No, what I said was that it's very important for the customer to want to buy the product. My God, what am I doing trying to have a rational conversation with a madwoman? Everyone told me I was crazy to put a woman in such a delicate position."

I decided to ignore the latter remark and to make my point.

"How can I make the customer want to buy something without showing what it does. How can I sell an insecticide without showing its effect on the ants, roaches, scorpions, and whatever else it is that this product is supposed to kill?"

He had no answer finally. But I could not help wondering why he was so upset. What did he mean when he said that he had put me in such a delicate position?

Finally he admitted, but under an oath of secrecy, that they were involved with the Chemical Company. The Chemical Company was the slang term used to designate the military installation where people said chemical weapons were being developed. When I heard the name, I was thunderstruck. For a moment, I could not say a thing. When I asked him angrily why he had not told me that we were working for the government, producing its propaganda, and that the agency was a front, he turned nasty on me.

"Don't act so innocent. We are in a war, you know. Everything we do is connected in some way to the war effort. That's only right and proper. Surely, you knew that?'

"No, I did not. Why should I? If it is connected and we're so proud of our patriotism and the war is good and just, then why don't we come out and say what it is that we're doing? Why do we hide? Why does the Chemical Company have to pretend it's producing insecticide? We should be proud that we are selling goods that can annihilate innocent civilians by the hundreds of thousands."

I was taken off the assignment.

Six years later, they gassed Halabja and the area around it. Sulaymaniya was my mother's hometown, where some of my cousins still lived.

In the summer of 1982, a college friend invited me to spend the summer on the Mediterranean. I needed a break and at that point I had saved quite a lot of money. So I went. First to London for a few days and then to Beirut.

Ah, Beirut. I got swept up by the intensity of this lovely city on the sea. It was burning, consuming itself from within, but from the air it looked as though nothing was happening. It was only when you got out of the plane and into a taxi and tried to move around the city that you got a sense of the violence and danger.

Roadblocks.

"Hawaytik! Your identity card!"

Crossings. The port. The museum. How to get from the west side to the east side without without too much danger or delay. It depended on the day whether what mattered was the danger or the delay. But what never changed was the downtown. The tall, gutted, burnt-out buildings whose black holes where windows had once been stared down at the passers-by. A shock on the first day, but by the third, just part of the new landscape.

Whatever they did, they did it 150%! When they had fun, they had lots of fun. Extravagant dinner parties, preferably in dangerous places so that it would be even more fun. There was a group of fear freaks, most of them foreigners who had come to Beirut to make their lives more interesting, who could not get enough of the adrenalin high. They founded the Dangerous Diners Club and made weekly expeditions to the most dangerous areas in town. Then there were the angry types, who would kill for the slightest reason. And for no reason. And lots and lots of people were writing, painting, making music, trying to make sense of it all, or trying to believe that something could be salvaged from the destruction. They created beautiful things, and ugly pornographic things with the same urgency. As though their lives depended on it.

I was staying with Great-Aunt Najwa in Ayn Mreissi. She'd moved from Haifa a few years earlier. Life in Beirut was so much freer than it had been in Baghdad. Everyone did what they felt like doing. But it reminded me of *Lord of the Flies*. Every day, a new Ralph would appear, the leader of a not-yet formed militia. Ralph had to have his Piggy to worship him and to be his brains. And his Jack, of course. So the militia began to take shape as The Family. Sometimes, walking down a street when things were suddenly quiet, unusually quiet, I could almost feel a bullet pass through my back and then be almost surprised that nothing had happened.

It was the end of May. Everyone was talking about an Israeli invasion that this time they were sure was going to happen. Aunt Najwa and I had been planning to go to the weekly salon at Galerie One. Every Friday night, come rain or shine, bombs or calm, writers and artists would converge on the art gallery on the east side of the city. There were poetry readings, art shows, or just great conversations about everything under the sun and, of course, lots of whiskey. Johnny Walker Black Label. For one evening a week, there was a truce and it did not matter what your religion or politics were as long as you were interested in art.

After leaving the gallery, where the conversation had been particularly lively, Aunt Najwa suggested that instead of going home we should go to the Commodore Hotel. The journalists, it seemed, had come to town, and she had added impishly "some in rags, some in tags and some in velvet gowns." They'd come from all over the world to Beirut to cover the long-awaited Israeli invasion. There were no confirmations but the alert was out and the international news agencies had sent in their correspondents.

Maryam told me about Arik and what he was doing while I was in Beirut, only a few miles away. I learned how he had tried to get his men to rebel and not to invade. How he had been punished. I had not even thought of the reality of the lives of the Israelis who were flying low over the Lebanese capital. They were evil. As we sat there under the bombs, we did not think of the individuals, just a faceless evil force.

"So who were they, these international experts?" Maryam asked.

Hardly experts! Parachute journalists more like it! We walked into the Commodore reception area and it was jammed with people, heavy with smoke. Aunt Najwa and I walked into the bar to meet with a friend of hers. We had not been there long when a slick character sitting at the bar started coming on to me, trying to impress me. He had just flown in from New Zealand. He'd never been to the Middle East. What an adventure! He tried to strike up a conversation with me, wanted to know where I was from. When he learned that I was not from there, he lost interest.

And when I asked him what he knew of the situation, he said, "nothing," but he wasn't worried because Beirut was "a piece of cake."

"A piece of cake!" No one I had met seemed to have any good idea what was happening and why, and they all lived there, had lived there since the beginning of the war seven years ago. One professor of political science at the American University had admitted that with all the political theory that he had had to absorb for his Ph.D. and that he was now ramming down his students' throats, he couldn't make heads nor tails of this war. He had dismissed it as a "postmodern war." Whatever that means, I had thought at the time but had not wanted to appear stupid by actually asking what that might mean.

Yet here was this arrogant jerk, straight from New Zealand or Tierra del Fuego or somewhere, who'd never spent more than a week in the Middle East and who was declaring with the boredom of an old Middle East hand that Beirut was a "piece of cake."

He told me that there were so many different versions to each event, you'd be crazy to think you could get the truth. So you just picked an informant, any informant. It didn't matter who, just so long as you stuck to this same person, so that the story would retain some consistency.

While I was listening, I noticed Peter, sitting two stools down the bar. He was staring at his beer, disconnected from all the swaggering around him. I was intrigued.

"Hi. My name's Hibba Lughod."

"Hi. Peter."

He was a stringer for a London-based Arab magazine and he, too, had no experience in the Middle East. He'd just come, without even thinking of turning down the assignment.

For some reason, I was not angry with him as I had been with the jerk a few minutes before.

"Have you ever covered a war?"

"Well, not quite."

"What d'you mean?"

He was silent. Afraid to lose his interest, I bumbled ahead. I asked him whether he had ever been in a war, and he said that he had. Where? Vietnam. Had he been a reporter? No, but he had written a novel about returning to some southern American town after his tour of duty in Southeast Asia and killing a guy. I'd read a novel just like that, I interrupted. By someone called Peter Hicks. On the trip to London, I had picked it up because of the rave reviews. Did he know the book? Yeah, he'd written it. I thought about the descriptions of the emptiness and desolation of peace, of beginning to lose his mind in the humdrum of reality at home, of killing to get high. He had not written of Nam, but it was there in every word that he wrote, more than it would have been had he written about the fighting, about the waiting in the jungle.

Suddenly, I felt shy. Not because he was a great writer and I was nobody. I was shy because of his long wild hair and unruly beard and tattered jeans and lumberjack shirt. His empty eyes flashed when he told me there was nothing he hated more than those halls filled with little old ladies who all wanted to know whether the stories he told were true. He would tell the Blue Rinse Brigade that of course they were true. And we both laughed because we remembered Tim O'Brien. Because the real "of course" is that there is no war story that is true except the one that is a lie.

"So, what was it like to be a god in the skies over Southeast Asia?" I asked.

And he answered that it was thrilling. That he'd never felt anything like it. That nothing could ever again be that exciting, not after flying so fast you felt you were still and the landscape peeled past like magic lantern shows.

"So you weren't afraid?"

"Afraid? No, no time to be afraid. Just tight."

It was almost painful to watch him relive those moments of unrelivable passion and excitement.

"Nothing since has come close. Not sex. Not marriage."

The life drained back out of his again dead face. He was again the cool reporter and I was shy again and a little bit afraid that I'd come too close. But I hadn't.

He was very tender. And I loved him that summer. That terrible summer of '82.

Maryam

May 1982

A voice was heard, boys, calling
The voice of my country and it said, My children,
I am your mother, I am Palestine
And I've been calling you for years.

The words of their song floated into the hospital room, and I thought of Hisham. He had been such a nice, quiet, bookish child. Now he was out there in the streets, with a gun on his hip. I'd asked him what he thought he was doing showing off the gun, did he want them to come in to the building and throw everyone out and take over the apartments?

"We're going to kick them out. We'll use every last stone, every last pebble to keep them away from us. Them with their M-16s and their jeeps and their tear gas. We can't go on submitting!"

His cheeks were flushed with excitement and I remembered Sitti's stories about the British and how she had fought them and what those years in their jails had done to her. And I thought about Usama. He would have been thirty-six, more than twice Hisham's age.

"We're learning in the streets. How to react when we see our brother beaten by the soldiers. How to behave. We're making our culture out of our reality, not out of books or study."

Hisham had learned indeed. Having given up the books, he was talking the talk.

Had I made the right choice? Was the future with Hisham? We had argued for a while, and I thought that he hadn't heard me, or that if he had he didn't care. But in the end, he did pull his shirt out of his pants and let it hang over the holster. A concession to Sitt Maryam. I was relieved but not fooled. I knew he would show off the new toy to his friends. However, whatever he did when he was with them, he never again strutted around the building with his gun showing.

I looked at my baby girl in awe. I smiled weakly at Arik who had not left my side throughout the two-day ordeal.

"Your mother called. She'll try again at six."

The nurse disappeared.

Arik turned on the radio. Mobilization to the North. Units were being called up. Would he have to go? The phone rang promptly at six.

"Maryam, *hayati*. How are you feeling? I miss you so much. I can't believe that I could not be there . . . your first baby . . . I'll come. I promise. I can't be long. I kept trying to call from the post office, but there were so many people waiting and I was afraid of waking you in the middle of the night. So Sitt Zulaykha allowed me to use her phone. What does Jamila look like?"

"How can you ask me! She is beautiful. Like her name."

"What color are her eyes? Her hair?"

"She is completely blonde . . ."

I felt light for an instant.

"Blonde!"

I could hear her mutter something to someone in the background. Then she was back, sounding even more nervous than before.

"Maryam, my heart, I love you. Baba kisses you."

"How's the job?"

"Good. Things didn't quite work out in the drafting department, so he's in another section now . . . Yes, Ma'am . . . Sorry . . . Of course . . . I've got to go. Oh, before I forget, Afaf sends her love. She's so excited about her new niece."

"How is she?"

I quickly interjected, knowing that this might be my last chance for a long while.

"She's going to be all right."

There it was.

After a pause, Mama was back on the line.

"May you bury me. Good-bye, *hayati*."

Click.

"Good bye . . ."

A little pang, and I pulled Jamila close to my heart. Would she live to bury *me*?

Assia

May, August 1982

"Good-bye, my life."

I was a grandmother. I had scarcely felt that I was a mother
and here I was a grandmother. Who was Jamila like? Me,
Maman, or Basil? Or dear Papa? Jamila. Beautiful. Yes. I liked the
name. Maryam had not forgotten the stories I'd told her about
the great Algerian heroines, Jamila Boupacha and Jamila
Buhrayd. Jamila will grow up to be a fighter. One cannot resist
one's name, right?

The Israeli invasion had turned out to be deeper and more
long-lasting than even the most pessimistic had anticipated.
After besieging Beirut for more than two months, they had
rounded up the Palestinian leadership and the various militias
and driven them out of the capital. Despite the humiliation of
the defeat, the young men refused to be cowed. Their defiant
victory signs allayed the anxiety we felt as we crowded around
Karim's television.

"Did you see that? Did you? The journalists are talking
about expulsion, defeat. . . Don't they have eyes in their heads

63

to see! Our boys are holding steadfast, *samidin*. Abu Ammar will never let us down."

"Hey, look at that Israeli officer. He thinks he's in charge. He has no idea. What do you say? Isn't it time for us to do something?"

Karim's eyes were shining as he turned to us. Basil and I looked at each other.

My heart was pounding painfully. It was not the first time I had felt this way. Each time I saw a group of my people being pushed around, humiliated and they would not lower their eyes, I felt this way. And when I looked at Basil, I saw the old light in his eyes and I loved him again and felt sad again. What were we doing here? I had believed Layla, and had persuaded him to travel for a cure. The streets, however, were not paved with gold, but with sand and salt. Sand that moved and salt that dissolved.

I could not bear to watch Basil go from job to job, adding something to the monthly check that I sent back even after Maman had died. It had been hard to learn that Maryam had married Arik. But she'd only done what we did. Married far from her mother without ceremony, without a party. Would she, too, turn up on our doorstep one day and want to live with us? Where would they live? What would they do? Who would look after the baby? Afaf? No, it was the three of us here. But some day . . .

I watched the black and white screen flickering on the formica countertop.

The rhetoric escalated and I knew that someday I'd have to leave. If not now, then soon.

"This cannot be taken lying down!"

"The PLO is not defeated!"

"Just take a look at those faces and the fists!"

"Basil, let's go back. What are we doing here? Fifteen years of living like dogs. We've nothing to lose."

Dream on, Karim. But don't forget your wooden leg.

"Come on, Basil, let's do it finally. Let's go back!"

Go back! Go back to what? I said nothing. Basil, however, had been quite blunt.

"OK. How do you propose we go about it? Shall we fly? How about first class? Or will business do?"

Umar and Hasanayn giggled.

He could say hurtful things, yet they took it without flinching because it was Basil who had said it. Sometimes I felt that I needed to spend more time around Karim and the brothers so that I could remember the Basil I had married so many aeons ago.

I walked toward the water. It was early evening and the young men were already out in their cars. They would be spending the next few hours cruising up and down the wide boulevards, trying to keep themselves amused until dinner. Ferraris, Mazuratis, Lambourguinis raced each other at traffic lights that seem to have been arbitrarily placed on the corniche along the Gulf to give the impression of a city.

I crossed at one of the lights and headed north. I walked along the coast in the area designated for sports. Nannies from Sri Lanka and the Philippines out with children and babies in strollers, young women jogging in veils, macho guys in bright sweatshirts pulling themselves up on monkey bars. Then on past a fastfood fish restaurant, empty as always. Should I walk on to the beach club?

I looked at my watch for the first time since leaving Karim's. 6:30. Time to go home. I hadn't thought of Afaf all day. I turned back regretfully and, giving a last glance at the water, made my way back to Hawalli.

Afaf
August 6, 1990

He seemed lost, as though looking for a place to hide. So I took him in. I held his hand and brought him close and I looked in his eyes and saw mine. I looked for the fear but found none. Minutes passed like prisoners dragging stones. I sat with this stranger as though with a neighbor, a friend, my friend. Then he kissed me.

Assia

August 6, 1990

"Baaasil! Baaaasssilll! Help me! Please, please . . . Oh, dear God! Aaghhhhh . . . I killed him. I actually killed him. The bastard. He was on top of her. Oh, my God, Baasil! She was just a child, my little baby girl. Afaf, I had wanted you to bury me . . ."

Basil stood at the door, transfixed. I was huddled on the floor, tearing at the hair that had tumbled about my face when I had stripped off the head scarf. My body was shaking spasmodically. Slowly, I dragged myself across the floor to a dark pile in the corner. The only sound was the buzzing of the fat red flies. I reached Afaf's corner by the window. In a sudden burst of energy and strength, I stood up and started to tear at the pile, to drag at it. I pulled at something heavy that kept resisting my best efforts. Suddenly calm and businesslike, I turned to Basil. Curtly, I gave him instructions.

"Come here and help get this beast off her. You take hold of the leg. Here, grab it by the shoe and pull hard."

Basil did not move.

"I'll pull the other leg. No. It's better to do it with the top part."

I tussled with the dark mass, and then as though remembering what it was that I was doing, I let out a long shriek.

"Oh, my God, look at my hands. They're covered with blood! They stink. Everything stinks. Get him off herrrrrr!!!!!!"

Basil could not move. Blocking the little light that struggled to enter the door of the place we had called home for so long, he stood still and silent. As silent as Afaf had been from the instant the bomb had exploded.

I was in a frenzy. I had to pull body from body, unlock the embrace. That filthy soldier was lying on top of my baby.

Silently and in slow motion, Basil doubled over and vomited. He vomited over his new, secondhand pants. He vomited over the mat Afaf had washed that morning. And for the first time in his adult life, he wept. The years of tears Basil had repressed welled up out of the bowels of his memory.

Again, I was completely calm. Without looking at the sobbing, choking man squatting on the floor in his vomit, I stood up. I picked up the scarf I had ripped off and tied it automatically around my head. I stood up and walked woodenly out of the door. I had to get help. I had to get that animal off my daughter and out of the house.

There was no one in the streets. The siren had just sounded and the radios I was passing were announcing a curfew. *Mamnu` al-tajawwul*. I should not be out.

Finally, I got to Karim's building. I took the stairs two at a time. I pounded at his door.

"Who's there?" Karim's voice was small and quaking.

"It's me. Assia. Hurry!"

"My God, you scared me."

Karim quickly unbolted the door.

"Assia, what are you doing out in the streets?"

"Assia, what are you doing out in the streets? How many times do I have to tell you the same thing! You must wait in the hall until they come. What will they think if they find you outside waiting alone. Your mother will be very angry."

Two blue eyes twinkled beneath the wimple-crowned brow. I turned to Sister Anna guiltily. I knew I should have stayed with the other girls. But I was too excited. I was always too excited on Saturday when Maman and Papa came to Bethlehem to take me out for the day. In the morning, I would wake up before the others, long before. I would try to lie still until the sun was fully risen. The sound of the chickens clucking calmed me, but then when the cock crowed. . .

What were they all doing, just lying there? Couldn't they see that the day was almost half over? Finally, finally, the matins were rung and I bounded out of bed. I was always good on Saturdays. I must not make any mistakes. None at all, lest I risk the sisters' displeasure and forfeit my magic moments with Maman and Papa.

Keeping my excitement under control, I walked carefully to the washroom. Slowly, I washed my face and brushed my teeth and hair, trying to make the endless hours between now and their coming go by with as little waiting as possible. I assembled my black and white uniform and laid it out on the bed. Then I rifled through the drawer of my little bedside table for the little pink slip I only dared wear on Saturday when I was going out. Still, there were three hours to wait.

This particular Saturday had been especially tense. I was excited as always but I also felt something else. Something that I had no word for.

11:00 came and went and no one had come.

11:30.

12:00.

No. That was too much. I could not stay stuck to the hall chair when I felt I was about to burst with disappointment and anger and something like fear. Where were they? How could they be so late when they knew I was waiting?

I looked around me. Everyone had gone to lunch. I just had to go and check. I tiptoed down the long hallway, through the smell of turpentine to the convent entrance. No. There was no car. Nothing was moving under that hot September sun. I ventured further so that I could see the Church of the Nativity, and next to it St. Catherine's. Further still and I could see the Don Bosco.

Nobody was out. Odd. Usually, I could see the women hurrying home from the market, carrying their baskets heavy with vegetables for lunch.

Where was the lettuce man? Usually, Maman would tell Papa to stop the car at the foot of the hill so that she could pick out the best, fattest lettuce that the old Armenian had for sale.

"Khass. Khass. Ajmal khass fil alam li ajmal sittat Bayt Laham. Let-

tuce. Lettuce. The loveliest lettuce in the world for the loveliest ladies of Bethlehem. *Khass ajmal khass fil alam.*" Slowly, he pushed his wooden cart up the hill. That was around 11:30. So by now he should be here. By now he should be surrounded by the loveliest ladies in Bethlehem, each fighting with the next for the lovely lettuce that was never as lovely as the one Maman would have picked out half an hour earlier when he started his climb up the hill to the convent school.

"Assia, what are you doing out in the streets?" Sister Anna's voice washed over me like a warm wave.

"Sister Anna, where are my parents?"

"Did they say they'd come today?"

"But it's Saturday. They've never not come on Saturday."

"Maybe they thought that the bazaar was today. You know, we notified the parents of the charitable bazaar next Saturday, and asked them to come an hour later because it would take some time to set up."

"No, no. They know all about that, and anyhow they were planning to come early to help put the stuff out. They are bringing my brothers to see my needlework sampler that was chosen for the competition."

"I wonder if they were caught in the events."

Her voice trailed off.

"What do you mean—'caught in the events'?"

I was suddenly afraid as I repeated the nun's words. All of my disappointment and anger vanished in a flood of fear that almost drowned me.

"Don't worry, my child. I am sure they're coming."

"Sister Anna, I'm afraid. Please tell me that they're O.K. Don't let them be caught in the events."

I had no idea what "the events" meant except that it would not be good for them to be caught in them.

I started to cry. I was class captain, and yet I was crying. Sister Anna, usually a bit stiff and distant, put an awkward hand on my shaking shoulder and drew me back into the cool convent cloisters out of the heat of the whitewashed courtyard.

"Assia, what are you doing out in the streets? Didn't you hear the sirens and the radio announcements? You could have been killed!"

"Karim, you've got to come at once. Something terrible's happened."

"But we can't go anywhere. They'll kill us! They've already taken the brothers . . ."

"And they've killed Afaf and I've killed one of them. You've got to come."

"Oh, my God! OK. Let's go." Karim's automatic refrain. "Where's Basil?"

Ten minutes later, we were back at the apartment. Karim squinted. The change from the sun-soaked alley to the damp darkness of the room briefly blinded him.

"The Iraqis have been here! Phew! Can you smell it? Must be the smell everyone's talking about."

"Yes. One of them is still here."

I paused.

"At least, he was a few minutes ago. Basil? Basil, where are you? I've brought Karim."

Silence. I listened to the silence and all I could hear was the buzzing of the red flies. As my eyes adjusted to the dark, I realized that the pile of bodies in the corner had changed. Where was Basil? What had happened to the soldier's body? Had he managed to get rid of it in those few minutes while I was gone? Had it all been a dream? An unbelievable nightmare and Afaf was asleep in her corner on the floor?

"Maman, Maman! Where are you?"

My fitful sleep that night had been filled with nightmares.

Sister Anna had spent the whole evening with me waiting for some word. There had been a demonstration near the Aqsa Mosque. There was even talk of women marching. Nobody knew for sure whether the demonstration had been peaceful. Everybody knew that the British were ruthless. Sister Anna had survived the Great War in her holy oasis. There she had prayed night and day for an end to violence.

"It's not true! I hate you. How could you say such a thing?! You're horrible! I hate you! Where's Maman? Where's Papa? He can't have left without saying good-bye. I hate you . . ."

The angry screams turned into heavy sobs.

"I'll tell them how you hurt me. I hate it here. I want to go home. Maman, pleeeeease come and take me away!"

And I, the nine-year-old class captain, turned over and buried my burning face in the already wet pillow.

Sister Anna, who had stood at a distance from the Mother Superior and me, now approached the bed. Slowly and quietly, she told me the story. The British had killed over a hundred Palestinians and Papa was one of them. They had put Maman in jail. The elegant Samya Lughod whose salon, Sister Anna said, was known as far away as Nablus had been thrown in with common prisoners. The papers were reporting that Sitt Samya had gone to the British governor's home with some wives of community leaders. She had been the first to unveil, announcing: "To serve our homeland we shall take off our veil." The women had then presented the governor with a list of demands.

"Shshsh, child, everything's going to be all right. Stop crying, sweetheart. Please."

⚜️⚜️⚜️

"Afaf, everything's going to be alright. Shshsh, child, Baba'll be right back."

I leaned against the door frame to catch my breath. I felt dizzy and I slowly slid down until I was squatting in the shaft of light that penetrated only a few feet into the room. I let my eyes roam over the familiar space, always coming back to Afaf's corner, always surprised not to find the entangled bodies, the pale long leg with the brown brogue dangling. And the thick khaki back with the area of darkness spreading, radiating out from the still center of the kitchen knife handle. I looked. Afaf was there, curled in the corner next to the upturned chair. I looked again. Curled up like a large khaki embryo, but with her blank eyes wide open, staring straight at me. It was suddenly hard to see because I was caught by the stench. Basil's vomit, the soldier's shit, the sick sweetness of drying blood, and then that other smell. The smell that Saddam's men had brought with them. The stink of another war. Like a greasy film on a sheet of glass, that new smell clung to everything.

"Assia, I found Basil. He's going to be all right. I think it's best if I take him back to my place."

Karim stood outside, leaning toward me. His skin was ashen and he was trembling. His eyes were red and bulging. He was always so awkward and this time even more so. He's going to be all right. We're going to be all right. It all sounded so familiar, so familiarly untrue. And suddenly, it was like a thick brick wall breaking, cracking, crumbling into the black space deep down inside me.

"He's dead, isn't he?"

Wasn't that what "all right" really meant? What people had always told me when someone I loved was gone for good.

"Of course not. Just a bit shook up."

"So where is he? Let's go and see him."

Suddenly, I needed Basil, to be reassured, and to be comforted.

"No."

And then more firmly.

"No. You stay here until I return. I'll be right back."

This was surprising resolve from Karim, and I gave in, almost grateful not to have to worry about Basil. At least, not for the moment. Karim left, hopping along as fast as he could. Dear old Karim. He had somehow given me strength, not much, but enough to pick myself up and to go over to the corner.

"Afaf, my darling baby. I am sorry. I am so sorry!"

I took her limp body in my arms and stroked her short bleached hair. I started to rock back and forth, moaning.

"Oh, if only we hadn't come! If only we'd stayed! You were all right all along and I was wrong. You were fine, my beautiful baby girl-boy. You didn't need to get better. We've got to go back! I can't stand it any longer."

Another burst of energy seemed to come from nowhere and, dropping Afaf, I jumped up. I had to pack. No. First, I had to tidy up. Yes. I'd clean a bit. Then, I'd decide what to pack. Water. I needed some water. The place was filthy. I had to wash the floor. I took the bucket out from under the sink and turned on the tap. One drop. Then another . . . Then, nothing. Oh, my God! Not now. There couldn't be a water cut. That was too much. I tottered back to where Afaf was lying. What in the hell was I to do now? It was then that I noticed the little white plastic card. I had not seen it before because it had been tucked under Afaf's left leg. But when I'd held her, I must have moved it. I leaned down to pick it up. It looked like an identity card.

Aziz

October 1981

Secret Contracts Type no. (2) General Security
        General Index Card
        Curriculum Vitae
        File number 43,304
Tripartite Name: Aziz Salih Ahmad
Date of Birth: 5 November 1956
Profession: Fighter in the Popular Army
Activity: Violation of Women's Honor

She stared at the bright white card in disbelief.

"Hey, Umm Salih, wake up! You look as though you've just seen a ghost. Tell me, what does it say?"

Line by line, letter by letter, Sanaa read out what was written on my new identity card.

"I can't believe it, Aziz. Do you understand what this means?"

"What's this, Umm Salih?"

"Your new activity . . ."

"Well, to be honest, no."

I smiled and gave her arm a quick, affectionate squeeze.

"Don't be an idiot, Aziz! Didn't the officer tell you what your Activity was to be? Didn't he tell you that it was v-i-o-l-a-t-i-o-n o-f w-o-m-e-n-'s h-o-n-o-r!"

She spelled out each word carefully, only just holding herself from screaming.

"D'you know what that means??!"

Quietly, I repeated what I'd already said:

"Sanaa, *bayati*, I've already told you that I don't."

I looked across the table at her. She was calming down a bit.

"Aziz, please don't act stupid. You know that you could have asked for another assignment."

"Stop it."

God, I can't stand the woman! Who in the hell does she think she is!

"Stop calling me stupid!"

"So, if you're not stupid, then you know what violation of women's honor means, don't you? It means rape. RAPE!!"

Sanaa was out of control and not caring whether the servants heard her. She screamed and coughed as the word tore out of her body.

"RAPE. They are sending you to the glorious war to rape. Women like me, like your mother, like your sister, like the daughter we may have."

So that was what it was all about. That was why they'd called me a lucky fucker and told me I was more likely to get a medal and to live. But who knew? Was it really safe? What if the woman's husband . . . or brother . . . ? I was afraid.

I looked into the steely black beads and then down at the spittle string that had dried into a white pellet in the corner of her mouth. Then up to the thick gray scarf. Then down slowly taking in every detail of this body I loathe.

Six months, that's all it had taken. It had been so easy. Lucky, in fact, that I couldn't afford the bus ticket to the capital, and had taken the next ride out of the mountains to Alabrak, the place of miracles. A great-aunt of a friend had once gone there on a pilgrimage. She had gone with a group of women. Nine months later, all these women had given birth to boys. A miracle! Actually, I didn't believe in miracles except when I hoped they would happen to me. Even though at first I thought I'd made a mistake and should not have come, I was wrong. It was a kind of miracle. But that came later.

At first, I wanted to go home. But I had no money. So I got a job. I'd work until I had the bus fare to return home. Abulfaraj saved me.

Abulfaraj, the pimp, had been there at the bus station when I arrived. He was the only well-dressed person there. That was why I'd noticed him. After spending hours squeezed tight in a bus that bumped and jolted down the mountain road, we could not wait to get out. But then what? I had no idea where to go. I spent the first night on a bench in the park. Actually, only part of the night because it turned out to be the mosque beggar's bench. When he had seen off the last of the faithful after the last prayer, he had come home.

He was furious when he saw me and started to hit me with his long, thick stick.

How dare you! You dirty country bumpkin! Go home!

I didn't wait around for more and ran off. After wandering around for hours I followed my nose to a bakery and collapsed for the last hours of the dark on its threshold. Just before dawn, the baker came and took me in. He was a nice man. He gave me the first loaf of the day and offered me a job delivering bread. But all I wanted to do was to go home.

Yesterday, it had been urgent to leave. I was sure I would not miss my mother. All she did was scold me and make me work. As for my father! Who would have ever thought I would miss them! And so soon!

I went to the bus station and realized, of course, that the return was an impossible dream. Impossible, that is, until I had earned, or stolen, the money for the bus fare. God knows how long it had taken me to collect the downhill fare!

I was hanging around the station when Abulfaraj made an appearance.

Abulfaraj was a pro. He'd look at a prospect and figure out immediately what was the best fit. But even he was surprised by how quickly I adapted. I cut my hair. Well, no, I'd never tried to grow a mustache, but I'd be happy to try. It might suit. I surprised him. A natural. I had an eye for the wealthy ladies and no reluctance to approach any, however old or ugly. Abulfaraj was almost disappointed at my lack of discrimination.

"As handsome a man as you've become you should not squander your favors."

For weeks I forgot about going home. Or, rather, remembered why I'd left. I was having a ball.

But when I came to ask about Ali's lame daughter, he was aghast.

"No, Aziz, that's too much! D'you know who she is? D'you know who you are?"

A week later, there was to be a big reception at the palace, and Abulfaraj was to provide the sweets. There were so many that all hands were welcome and Abulfaraj forgot to forbid me from going.

She was flushed as she rushed around, making sure that the soup tasted good and the flowers were just so. I watched her from the door, hiding behind the pile of cakes and cookies. Someone asked her what to do with the sweets. She was looking for a safe, cool place when our eyes met. She blushed and was suddenly flustered.

"Put them over there. No. Take them to the pantry. Oh, there's no room. I don't know. Never mind. Put them anywhere."

I loved it, that moment of power when I knew I had her where I wanted her. I was nobody, but I'd made this rich, powerful woman confused and helpless.

I reminded her of that day.

"Remember, the party? You were so lovely. I love you when you're gentle."

She strode up and down the room in her gray woolen overcoat and fanned herself in the heat that the air-conditioning unit could not combat. Just after we married, I told her that I'd really prefer it if she'd cover. And she did. Just like that. She'd do anything I asked.

She stopped, and I knew that, for the time being at least, I was back in charge.

Afaf

August 6, 1990

He seemed lost as though looking for a place to hide. I sat with this stranger as though with a neighbor, a friend, my friend. My first friend. And then he kissed me. Gently, his lips brushed my brows, my eyes. I touched his arm, his shoulder, his neck. I touched the skin of his neck. He was trembling.

Aziz

May 1982

A few months later, I was back on leave.

"No, there were no women there. The front is a dirty, dangerous place and there are no women anywhere near. By the way, you were wrong."

He paused meaningfully.

"The job title does not mean what you thought it meant. Violation of Women's Honor does not mean rape."

"So what does it mean?"

"It means turning the enemy into women and then violating their honor by killing them."

She knew that I knew that she knew I was lying.

The family was beginning to be proud of the son-in-law and to bask in borrowed glory. They were doing their bit for their country.

Maryam

May 1982

I held Jamila close, kissing the baby's soft, blonde hair.

"Maryam, I'm going to have to go."

"What d'you mean? I thought you'd told them you couldn't go."

"My unit depends on me."

"So do Jamila and I. You have new responsibilities. Besides, you'd promised. Why have you changed your mind?"

"I've given the matter lots of thought. What good do I do anyone if I hide away and protest to you and the walls? I think I have a chance to do something now."

"Do what?! Kill my people?"

I was almost shouting.

Suha called from the hall. Did I want anything from the market? She was really something, always appearing when we raised our voices. Did she keep her ear permanently at the keyhole?

"Thanks, Suha. We're fine. We've still got the *mulukhiya* you brought over yesterday."

I had gone to the door.

"Everything OK?"

Suha peered through the crack in the door, trying to see what was going on.

"Fine. Thanks for asking."

"How's the baby?"

Suha had inched closer to get a better angle on the room.

"Sleeping. I promise I'll bring her over when she's better. She's a bit delicate now."

"May God take care of her."

Suha gave up and withdrew.

"Can we go on living like this? Hiding from others . . . from ourselves?"

Arik was glum.

"What do you propose we do? We can't let the neighbors know. It was hard enough trying to convince the Association . . . and everyone there, at least, was sympathetic . . . But these Suhas. . . ."

My voice trailed off. Jamila had started to cry. Every time I heard the baby cry, I was afraid something was wrong.

I thought back two years when I was in my second year of teaching at the Hebrew University. It was a terribly difficult time. I was constantly worrying about my decision to accept a job inside. Always trying to convince myself that this was the way to make a difference.

That was when we had first met. It was the university cafeteria. I had overheard an argument at the next table. A tall, tanned man with blonde hair and intense blue eyes was pounding his fist on the sticky table to make his point. He had apparently just returned from Egypt where he had had discussions with students at

Cairo University. He was trying to tell his friends what it had been like, how these students had spoken better English than he did, how difficult it had been for them to think about being at peace with Israel, how the whole Arab world was rejecting them because of Camp David, how the meeting had made all of them realize that the biggest part of the problem was ignorance. But the more the blonde man insisted, the more his companions resisted. They were outraged at his proposal that they approach some of the Arab students and professors to see whether they might not be willing to work together. For these Israeli students fresh out of the army and indoctrination, we were not quite human. They acted as though they did not see us. I knew.

However, this young man was different. I'd heard liberal types go on and on about joint action, but then immediately back down when it came to joint condemnation of the government. The Arabs might condemn the PLO, but the Israelis would not do the same for their government. Wasn't it enough that two years ago they had signed a peace treaty with Egypt? Yes, he was very different.

Aware of the risk I was taking, I went over to him. I introduced myself to the students.

"Hello, I am Professor Maryam Lughod."

They seemed startled. My Hebrew was good.

"I couldn't help overhearing your conversation. May I join you?"

"Please, take a seat."

They smiled awkwardly, but they did not stay long. One by one, they trickled off, with some lame excuse or other. But Arik had stayed, and we had talked for a while. There had to be a way for the students to get together. At four, I had to go and teach.

"It was good to meet you."

"Wait. Could we talk again? I am really serious about organizing a student association. But I can't do it alone. Would you consider being the faculty advisor if I can get something going?"

"Sure. Let's talk. I usually have lunch here around one. We could meet tomorrow, if you like."

We met the next day and the next and the next. I found myself awaiting our lunch meetings with excitement. I was somewhat afraid of my feelings. At first, I convinced myself that I was attracted to what he said and how he said it. His cool blue eyes would flash as he dreamed out loud about the kind of place Israel could become. I found myself blushing whenever he asked me a question, realizing that I had not paid full attention to what he was saying. He seemed crestfallen, probably taking my absent-mindedness to be lack of interest.

To take the situation in hand, I decided to change the routine.

We had been meeting for lunch every day at the same time and in the same place for two weeks. Even over the weekend. All of my previous anxieties were nothing next to this!

I began to fantasize about him in bed. After trying to suppress his image, I would give in and imagine the first kiss. I would be walking through an alley just below the university, when he would appear. He would look distracted, sad even, but when he saw me he would light up, hurry his step, stretch out his hand in greeting, feel my willingness, pull my hand his chest and envelop me in his strong arms . . .

Cut!

An alternative scenario was in the university. The weekend when most of the students were at home. I'd be in the library, working in a carrel so deep in concentration that I was oblivious to the world, when suddenly I would feel a light touch on the nape of my neck . . .

Cut!

Yes. I had had to change the routine. To make sure I'd not lost my mind, I decided to introduce Arik to some of my friends. Test their reaction. For about six months, I had been working with some of my students in the hopes of opening a "college." I had offered the apartment. It was too big for me, too empty after Sitti had died. They recruited five professors from Birzeit and Najah. We worked on the curriculum which would include history, psychology, sociology, Arabic literature and political science. The students were to be boys and girls who wanted a degree while remaining involved. There had been some talk about inviting one or two Israelis.

They had liked Arik. He was studying Islamic history at the university. Within a couple of days of our meeting, he had started to audit my Arabic literature class and his passion for the poetry was contagious. He made me believe again in what I was doing. I was reminded why I had chosen to teach at the Hebrew University and not at Jerusalem University or at Birzeit. I hoped to make my Israeli students understand and eventually respect and admire the culture of a people whose existence their government was trying to erase.

"I've decided to take a public stand."

"About what? Us?"

"No. About the invasion. And I can't do it here. I have to go to my unit. I have to speak to my men. I have to make them understand how wrong this is. If we go into Lebanon, we won't get out like we did from Entebbe. It's a quagmire. Everyone knows it's a quagmire. That's what they call it."

Arik paused, and then continued as though talking to himself.

"What do they think they're going to get out of this crazy, wicked venture? They used to lecture us about Lebanon and the tribal fueds beneath its veneer of a modern Westernized society. They told us that the only campaign that would succeed in Lebanon was an air campaign. Surgical strikes. Like 1969. They were so proud of the summer of '69. Targeted and hit seven Middle East Airlines jets on the Beirut airport runways and withdrew without attracting fire. Job well done!"

Arik paused again.

Jamila was crying.

I looked at him.

Had I married the enemy?

"But now we're going in by land. The Americans must be behind this."

Arik then told me what he was planning. He was going to join his men as though ready to join the invasion forces and then he was going to refuse to fight. His men, trained to absolute obedience, would follow his lead. Hopefully, their example would inspire others. Mutiny on the Bounty . . .

Afaf
August 6, 1990

I am inside, yet as though outside. The warm, fragrant water holds me safe. She's bustling about the bathroom, arranging the roses, muttering to herself. Now and again, she approaches, stops and then walks off again. She's killed him. Yes, she killed him without even checking who he was or what he was doing. She killed him, my friend. Where's Father? What did he do with him?

Karim

August 6, 1990

"Basil, we've got to leave this place! Why in the hell did you drag that soldier here?"

Basil shot me a suspicious look, then squatted and stared into the desert.

"Come on, man. Let's go to Assia. She's going to be worried."

I started to pull at Basil's sleeve. But he'd withdrawn into a world all his own. He startled babbling as though talking to someone else.

"Oh, my little girl. How could it happen again? I am not a man . . . I ran away . . . Men don't run away . . . I should have stayed and died fighting . . . Basil, you're a coward. A worthless coward. Even when you held him in your arms—when you thought you could protect Usama—they got him, and you lived on."

He sneered and went on.

"You should have died . . . I wish you'd died . . . I wish I'd died . . ."

Basil started to pound his body in fury. I grabbed hold of his flailing arms.

"Hey! Take it easy! You're going to hurt yourself!"

"Who cares!"

I felt that Basil knew who he was again, so I took advantage of the moment.

"Basil, let's go back to Assia."

"No, I can't . . . I can never go back to her . . . not after killing both her children!"

"Don't be crazy, man! You didn't kill them. The Israelis killed Usama and the Iraqi pig killed Afaf. You did your best."

I didn't know what to add, so I said, "You couldn't do anything else."

I went on mouthing comforting words in the hopes I might get Basil to move away from the foul-smelling corpse. The mangled flesh was beginning to attract swarms of fat red flies. I did not remember having ever seen these red flies before.

"Basil, it's getting dark. *Yallah*, Ammu! Come on, my friend, let's get going!"

What should I do? I wasn't strong enough to carry Basil, who was a big man. Six foot two and almost 200 pounds. I could support him if he was willing, but if he resisted, I wouldn't be able to keep my balance. I couldn't budge him an inch. Finally, I decided to go for help. At first, I moved off slowly looking back with every step. Basil didn't move. Then I broke into a run.

I rushed to Basil's house. No one was there. Then to the cafe. Empty also. Then to Umar and Hasanayn's house. Again, no one. Of course, I'd forgotten, the Iraqis had taken them.

There was no one anywhere. The streets were empty. I knew I was in danger, but I also knew I had to get help for Basil.

Taking the back streets, I made my way cautiously to Sitt Zulaykha's palace. Why was it that crises always happened at the height of summer? It was the 6th of August and even though the sun was down, the heat was held in the walls and the ground. I could feel it penetrate my body through my foot.

Why did Saddam want to invade? What were his men doing down in Hawalli? On the radio, it had sounded as though he was challenging America. That was good. But then there was this dead Iraqi soldier at the city dump with Basil. That was not good. And the men who had picked up Hasanayn and Umar. People were saying that Saddam was wanting to put the Kuwaitis in their place, cut them down to size. Good. But there were some who thought that he wanted to go farther and invade Saudi Arabia and take over the Peninsula oil and become another Nasser. That would be good as long as Saddam liked the Palestinians. So why were they in Hawalli? I thought that I would listen to a radio as soon as I got help for Basil.

Finally, I caught sight of the palaces at the end of the road. The four identical palaces stood in a mile-long line. They were well known. People would come just to look at them. Tourists from the ships passing through the Gulf from India on their way to Basra would take taxis from the harbor to go and gawk: Was it really true that each wife had exactly the same house, the very same clothes? Why was that?

There was a flash of flame in the sky above the third palace. Then I noticed the smoke. A black cloud hung heavily over the palaces, with its thickest concentration in the middle. Something was wrong. I didn't know what to do. I was afraid to go ahead, knowing that the Iraqis must be there. But I was also afraid to return. So I decided to go to the Palestinian Embassy in Hawalli.

Maryam

July 1990

Eventually, I read about Arik in the *International Herald Tribune*. The Israeli and Jordanian papers did not carry the story. At least, not for a long time. Jamila did not get to see her father until she was five years old.

They'd taken care of him, made sure he would not do that again. Ever. But these marks they had gouged into his flesh were signs of his refusal, out there in the open for all to see. He no longer had to hide.

He was released in December of 1987, just before the Occupied Territories burst into open rebellion. The military authorities must have known they would need all the cells they could lay their hands on. And anyway, Lebanon was history. Five years had passed.

For months, Arik refused to speak about what had happened. But with time, I was able to piece together the story. Arik had joined his unit at a camp just north of Haifa. He was briefed. The ground troops were to advance just as far as a line drawn 40 kilometers north of the border. No, the commanders had insisted, they were not going to Beirut. What mattered was gaining control of the areas out of which the Palestinians were operating.

"All along it sounded like we were going to Beirut. After all, PLO headquarters were in the Lebanese capital. So what was the 40K-line story? Carefully, I considered my strategy. Should I talk to the men here in Israel, disable the process from the start, or should I wait until we were in Lebanon and the eye of the world was on us and our maneuvers? I decided to wait. Although I was pretty sure my men would obey me, I was afraid that on home territory the mutiny could be more easily coopted. It was more likely that the brushfire would spread when we were in the field.

"We were amazed at the reception as we pushed beyond the border and into the villages of the south. It was like a knife into butter. No opposition. Far from it. The women came out into the streets, their arms filled with flowers. They threw the flowers onto the tanks, placed wreaths around our necks. Nobody'd expected this, least of all I. But then the honeymoon ended abruptly. Of course, we didn't stop at the Litani. The PLO was in Beirut, dummies! Ah, of course . . ."

That was when Arik had acted. He learned, however, that the vaunted discipline was not what he had thought it would be. The men under his command did not obey him the moment he slipped out of his military role. He was immediately shipped out of Lebanon and sent to the Negev desert command. After a quick trial, he found himself in a top-security jail, Ansar III. There had been some discussion about where he was to be kept. Should he go to the section reserved for the common criminals, or for political prisoners, or should he be thrown in with the

"Arabs"? The officials decided that he should spend a spell with
each. The prisoners would take care of him as well if not better
than the jailers.

One hot July day, almost three years later, he told me what
had happened, and I understood why it had been so hard.

"They were animals, Maryam. Animals. There were eight of
us in this one cell. Eight bunk beds in a tiny space. Hardly any
room to move and only a couple of sitting areas. As soon as I arrived I knew that they had been told my history. They stood in a
line. Seven thieves, murderers, rapists, embezzlers were placed
in judgment over me and given free license to do what they
wanted. The guards threw me to the ground and I was at their
feet. All I could hear was the pounding of my heart. I don't know
what I'd expected, but it wasn't this. Solitary confinement perhaps. Or a section for political prisoners. Somehow, I'd never
imagined myself ending up with such a group. Then the silence
was broken by the sound of spitting. I felt their saliva hit and
trickle over my head as they chanted: "Arab lover. Traitor. Arab
lover. Traitor." Then they started to kick me. Then. . . ."

Arik could not continue. He had choked on the memories
that flooded out his voice. I came to where he was sitting on the
sofa and put my arm around his shoulders. I didn't know what to
say. It had taken him almost three years to be able to speak about
his time in prison. He had told me everything else. Several
times. But always, just as he was about to go beyond the trial, he
would stop. I'd never asked.

"Arik, it's all right. You don't have to tell me . . ."

I almost dreaded hearing what he had to say.

"No. I've got to. Otherwise, it'll stay with me forever."

He pulled himself together and continued steadily.

" Then their ringleader, an ugly bald guy with tattoos on his arms that he liked to ripple when angry, whispered menacingly: 'Fucked an Arab, Arab lover? What was it like? Go on, tell us. Tell us. Tell us.' The men chanted with him: Tell us. Tell us. When I wouldn't answer, he kept on repeating himself, but louder and louder. The echos of his screams bounced around the cell and then kicked down onto me. 'Hey, brothers, you heard anything?' He'd turned to the others and they replied that no, they hadn't. 'Now that's a shame, because we'd like to know, wouldn't we, boys?' And they all nodded and said, 'Yeah!' and looked at each other with knowing nods and winks. 'Look here, traitor, if you're not going to tell us, we're just going to have to find out for ourselves, aren't we, brothers?' And again, they nodded and said they would. Suddenly, they fell on me, like dogs on a fox. I thought they were going to kill me . . . and then . . . I wished they had . . ."

Again, Arik stopped and looked at me, his eyes imploring me to understand so that he wouldn't have to say anything, wouldn't have to put into words the horror of what he had been through. But this time, I needed to know.

"What happened, *habibi*?"

I knew that I knew, but wanted to be told that it was not so. Arik leaned forward, his elbows on his knees, his head in his hands. He looked as though he was trying to work out a puzzle. His voice was muffled.

" The bald guy, his name was Shlomo, stopped them and

grabbed me by the collar. He dragged me up off the ground and over to one of the bunks. He smashed my face against the back of the top bunk and pinned me in place."

Arik's voice changed into a monotone, as though he were reciting a lesson he'd learned by heart, but hadn't understood.

"One of . . . them yanked my belt . . . off and pulled . . . at my pants the button . . . popped he . . .   put his arm around my waist from behind and opened the zipper so . . . that the pants slipped . . . down to the floor he was still holding . . . me close closer to him and then I felt his thing and he was inside me and I felt nothing and they were . . . shouting what's it like to fuck an Arab lover and he . . . was shouting that it was . . . great you should try and . . . they did . . . one after the other . . . after the other . . . after the other after the other after the . . ."

I sat stock still, staring into his stony gaunt face. The silence lasted for a full minute, and it seemed that Arik was done. He slumped in his seat and he looked suddenly old, his blue eyes vacant.

I thought of the old people I'd seen in the nursing home where Sitti had spent the last month of her life. Around mealtimes, those who were well enough would be wheeled into the dining room where they would be placed around tables that could accommodate six wheelchairs. While they waited for the nurses to bring the food, they sat there in total silence staring glassily ahead. The only sound would be the television, cheerfully offering some commodity or other for the viewer's delight or recounting some disaster from the world. Thank heavens for the television, I'd often thought. I would chat away with Sitti, try to strike up a conversation with one of the neighboring wheelchair occupants, but with little success. I would then turn my attention to the television, grateful for its artificial cheer. But, now and here, there was no television, just a terrible silence and this specter.

I pulled myself out of my torpor and put my arms around the suddenly small man, feeling for him the tenderness of a mother but also of a daughter for her helpless father.

Later, piece by piece, I fitted together the remaining pieces of the jigsaw. Arik had lasted only a week in the criminals' cell. Even the authorities who had wanted the prisoners to do their job for them had been shocked at their viciousness. They did not have a mandate to execute him so they were compelled to remove him. After a week in the infirmary, where they patched him up, they sent him to the Arab section. It was there that he had met Shadeed, the fighter who had been tortured into madness. Everyone admired Shadeed. No one had lasted as long. Arik had observed him from a distance. Over the weeks, he had watched him collapse into the shell of himself. And then, one morning Shadeed was gone.

Aziz
May 1990

"When we fear nobody but God as we move toward unity; and when we depend on our peoples and nation, which have proved capable of shouldering their responsibility under extremely complicated circumstances—only then we can guarantee for ourselves a strength that knows no weakness, that does not abandon established rights, that can look confidently toward a better future, and that can restore every lost right—especially our right to dear Palestine, which is waiting impatiently to see Arab flags, especially the Palestinian flag, flying over it and over the domes of holy Jerusalem."

I switched the television back to the VCR. Words. Nothing but words. Saddam keeps on inviting in foreign dignitaries, holding extraordinary Arab summits in Baghdad, and blustering on about Palestine, wishing it and its people and their struggle, their "just struggle against the Zionist aggression and occupation" glory and mercy.

What about his promises to his soldiers? Where's our reward?

I have to get Hibba back.

"Where are you off to so soon?" Sanaa asked.

"To make sure everything's under control."

"No, I can't do business from home. No, it's not enough to give a call. I have to see for myself.

"No, Sanaa dearest, the journey is so tiring and you know how the pollution gets to you. I'll be back as soon as I can."

I left, carrying papers and documents and a preoccupied look. The minute I set foot inside the apartment, I called Hibba. No answer. Was she never home? Or, was she no longer answering the phone?

It had been terribly hot. The sun beat down through a gray haze. My clothes stuck to me. And I was sick with fear. The men were excited and they had surged forward. I lingered, not eager to be in the vanguard. I let the others go ahead and hid under some brush. It was so quiet in the village, eerily quiet. What if I was surrounded and the enemy was about to jump out and attack? I thought I felt eyes on my back. All over my body. But nothing moved in the hot stillness. The sweat trickled down through my hair and into my eyes.

I had to find a better place once I was sure there was no one there. I had to get out of the sun. Not far from where I was lying there was a hut that to seemed safe enough. I held my breath trying to decide what to do. Was it better to stay here or should I go to the hut? What would the men think if they returned or found me lying on the ground? I could pretend to be hurt. But if I stayed where I was, the heat might kill me.

I was dizzy. The heat was making it impossible to think.

Was I more afraid of the Iranians, or of the scorn of the men or of the sun?

I dragged himself slowly toward the hut.

Russian roulette. Would this be the one chamber holding a bullet?

Not a sound.

Nothing.

Even nature, it seemed, had stopped breathing in this heat. Inch by inch, I pulled myself over to the door and into the dark, cool space. At first, I could see nothing. Not a single ray of the white light that had blinded me outdoors. I sat back against the wall, daring for the first time to fill my lungs.

Suddenly, I realized that I was not alone.

In the corner lay an old man, paralyzed with fear. The fear flooded back, but I knew that I had to do something. My duty? I decided to use the gun for the first time in seven years of service. I aimed. My eye caught the old man's and I felt as though I knew the look. The man must have been in his seventies.

I tried to pull myself together and to fire. But the old man's terrified look had turned into a questioning gaze. He was look-ing at me the way father had looked at me a long time ago when I was about to do some mischief and he knew what it was even before I had clearly worked out what it was to be. That look had never stopped me from doing whatever was on my mind, but it had stayed with me throughout the mischief. And afterward. I had never felt alone, private. Even after he died, I felt his pres-ence and the need to defy it. So here he was again, but in the body of an enemy. A legitimate target. I could finally destroy the specter that had haunted me throughout my life. And serve my country!

My trembling hand steadied as I pointed the barrel at a spot between the old man's eyes. As before, I defied the look, the rebuke. Bang! I hit the chest. Bang! The cheek. Bang! The belly. I kept shooting at father. But he would not die. He had crumpled even further into the corner, his head sunk so deep into his shoulders that it seemed swallowed up, but the eyes. . . . Yes, the eyes remained open. They were no longer frightened, nor questioning. They were filled with contempt. I knew that look. Oh, God! How often had I forced myself not to be weakened by the old man's scorn. How often had I killed him before I killed him. But this time was harder than all those other times. This time, I knew that if I did not destroy this man, father would survive to judge me, to enter my head and make me accountable for the mischief I made.

This time, I had to come close to the wreck I was making, I had to be near enough so that the cold of the metal could touch the wizened face. With the dread of the devil crushing my heart, I put out one of the scorn-filled eyes. Then the next. I was so close that the blood out of the exploding eye spattered my khaki.

Later that afternoon, the unit assembled. Every man had a story to tell. Each had done his duty by fucking at least one enemy bitch! With the ones who resisted the most, they had agreed on an alternative strategy. Let the whole unit have her. When the excitement had died down, someone turned to me.

"Just a minute, angel-face, where were you?"

"I was there."

"Ahmad, did you see Aziz? Who saw Aziz?"

All the faces in the room turned to me. Where had I been?

Sweat broke out all over my body. It beaded on my brow and started to trickle down the temples and into my eyes. Impatiently, I wiped my face while trying to maintain a semblance of calm.

"What's with you, guys? I was with you until we got to that second house. Then, I went in there and did some business of my own."

"I bet you didn't do anything. Bloody coward. Afraid the clubfoot might not let you into her bed?"

And they all burst out laughing. They knew about Sanaa and how well I lived and they hated me for having what they wanted. Well, not the cripple of course, but all the rest.

I never told anyone about the old man in the hut, vowing never again to be freaked out by an old man in a hut. Maybe father had been right when he insisted that the only good death was in war, and that to die in war as a hero one has to stand to the last. Even if the enemy is there before you, shooting straight at you, you have to hold your place and your head. Nothing worse than being shot from behind, father had sneered. Father, however, had died of syphilis. So it was up to me to live out his dream. I needed another war, but a better war.

When I heard Saddam's statement to the Arab Summit, I was happy. Good for business, but good also for me. All the films I'd watched had taught me an important lesson I'd not known when I'd joined the Popular Army. If you were a real hero, truly brave, why you survived!

By the time I returned home on leave, my story had become

quite elaborate, with swarms of fierce Iranians and me, the bionic man. Everyone believed me. Everyone, that is, except for Sanaa. Oh, and of course, Hibba.

The bitch had left without saying good-bye, just when I was beginning to love her.

Maryam

August 5, 1990

The phone rang. From where I sat, I could see the street that runs in front of the National Palace Hotel. There were lots of people milling around the entrance. They must be having another conference, I thought. Though people looked more nervous now. Lots of little groups huddled together. Things were getting tenser by the day. Saddam Hussein had invaded Kuwait three days ago and no one, not even CNN, seemed to know what was going on.

"You can leave the paper with the secretary because I won't be going to the university today."

"No, on second thought, don't bother. I'll give you an extension."

I returned to the sofa. I was jumpy. Every time the phone rang I thought it would bring some news of them. I had never felt so remote and yet so very close. I surfed the TV channels looking for some coverage of events in the Gulf. I don't know what I was expecting to find.

"These students are something! I could give them a deadline

that was a year away and they'd have some great excuse to get the paper in late."

"Why do you accept late submissions? Aren't you too lenient?"

I responded immediately: "No. I don't really care about the deadline as long as the work is good."

Arik had just returned from the library.

"Have you heard anything?"

"Situation's not changed in the last hour. Maryam, sweetheart, don't fret so much. I know it's hard but if anything had happened to them, I'm sure we would have heard."

"How? Arik, you know whenever I think of them I can't imagine them with friends or anyone. What if the Iraqis have already gotten to Hawalli . . ."

I looked up and saw Arik watching me tenderly. He went to the kitchen, and a few minutes later returned carrying a tray with two glasses and a bottle of red wine.

"I don't want my love to be sad. Here! Let's drink to your parents!"

"And to Afaf!"

I smiled. It was probably better to drink a bit. Just to calm down, especially since there was nothing else to. He had just the right touch, gentle, jocular.

"Cheers!"

"Cheers!"

I sipped some wine, allowed it to linger on my tongue so as to taste its full richness and then slowly swallowed it.

"Mmmm . . . delicious. . . . What is it?"

"Ksara."

"Of course, the best! D'you know what would be perfect?"

"Falafel."

"Mind reader!"

Arik smiled. It was 5:30, and the falafel vendor had, by the smell of things, just set himself up at the street corner. The breeze was blowing in our direction and it brought with it the warm smell of spicy, bubbling oil. Arik slipped out, and a few minutes later returned with a small newspaper-wrapped package. He took a small, square, blue-painted plate out of the cupboard and then placed the hot, fragrant patties around the edge. In the center, he put a small bowl with the same blue design as the plate, and poured a creamy, tangy, garlicky sesame sauce into it. He fetched some olives and pickles from the larder and refreshed our drinks. I curled my legs up under me.

"Obviously, I can't stop thinking about them. Particularly Afaf. I remember the time when she was eight, Jamila's age. My parents had talked a great deal about her education. Would it be good to send her to school with other kids as though there were nothing wrong with her, or should she be spared the possibility that the kids would find her odd and torment her? Should they teach her what they could themselves? Sitti had suggested that they might bring in a tutor. Maybe they should send her to that school outside Jerusalem for deaf and dumb children? The discussions would turn into arguments and then shouting matches and then sad reconciliations. The outcome was that Afaf stayed at home and we all taught her something. I taught her the Arabic alphabet and then the English. Baba taught her math. It was odd how much he was with her. When she seemed able to read, Mama gave her some history lessons. She used the book I'd had at school. Afaf learned quickly, absorbed everything we pre-

sented to her. But without joy. We got used to her vigilant pres-
ence. It was clear she was noticing everything, but we had no
idea what she was making of it all."

I sipped my wine and then bit into a falafel I had dipped into
the sesame sauce. So fresh and warm and comforting. For a fleet-
ing second, I had a vision of Sitti picking through the little pile
of chickpea patties looking for the one with the most appealing
shape, the one that had been "fried just right for me," as she
would always say when criticized for spending too long and
touching too many when we were waiting our turn.

"Ah! Amm Khalil really is the best. *Ma fi hada mitlu!*"

And she would sigh and close her eyes contentedly. That
was how I liked to remember her.

"Afaf understood everything."

I remembered her paintings. The tent with the eyes. And
the kids throwing stones. Over the years these images came
true, if you can say that images come true. I must have been
quiet for a while, because I felt Arik fidget:

"How d'you know?"

"I've told you how she liked to paint. But when I think about
it, it seems as though she was always painting what was to
come."

I told him about the eyes in the tent.

"Do you think Afaf's clairvoyant?"

That sounded trite and inappropriate, more like how you
might describe an old woman with long, black-dyed hair, wild
old eyes and a crystal ball turning between thick-knuckled fingers. But there had been something of the seashore soothsayer
in Afaf. I remembered the violence I had felt in her paintings.

"When the Intifada broke out three years ago, and even before as the Resistance was gathering momentum, I had the same sense of eerie recognition I had had in September of 1982 when we got smuggled copies of international papers and saw the pictures of the Sabra and Shatila massacres.

"The drawings were so explicit, it was as though Afaf had traveled forward in time and found these horrifying images. But the faces in the pictures were ours: mine, Mama's, Baba's, Sitti's, Afaf's. Yes, she had filled the drawings and paintings with self-portraits. We were all there in those nightmares.

"The watercolors were often set in our neighborhood. But she had filled our then-quiet Jerusalem back streets with Israeli soldiers and tanks, bearing the blue and white flag. In some drawings, the uniformed men were walking, in others they were slouched against a wall, in others sitting on a tank. The children were wearing kaffiyehs that only the old men at that time used to wear. They were wearing them wrapped around their heads just like the *shabab* do it today, with just a slit for the eyes. Afaf had painted our future long before it became our present reality.

"There was a black canvas among the paintings that would have provided the finishing touch. It was the only oil I'd ever seen her do. It's a little room. The walls are black, though streaked with red, green, and a very little white. In the corner is a window with bars. Under the window is a heap of something. I couldn't make it out. The colors were a bit muddy, as though she couldn't get it quite right. But as I kept looking, I started to make things out. Two heads. One in profile, the other from the back. A woman and a man. Almost as though they were making love, but not quite. I remember being a bit shocked, as though Afaf shouldn't have known about that kind of stuff. After all, her name did mean Chastity! Then, I got annoyed. How dare she think such thoughts, let alone paint them! Seeing that I was displeased, she quickly rolled up the canvas and almost ran out of the room. I couldn't sleep that night."

I paused.

"And now, it's the same. I've not been able to sleep for a week."

"I know." Arik murmured.

The doorbell rang. Hibba was back.

Assia

August 6, 1990

I poured some more warm water on her face. Straining under the weight of the sodden body, I tried in vain to lift it up out of the tub. Why was it so heavy? Why could I not carry this infant of my womb? Had I not done so for nine months and not so long ago?

I stopped struggling and knelt by the tub. I stared at Afaf. The cropped blonde hair that framed her still adolescent face was flattened dark by the water. The features were distinct. If I were to touch it, I would know that this was not the skin of my daughter's face. I wanted to peel away this rubber cover. Gingerly, with the tips of my fingers, I brushed the face and the body I had been frantically scrubbing for the past thirty minutes.

I was suddenly struck by the reality of this body. Was she dead? There was no blood. My God, could it be that she was in another of her fits? I had to do something about it. Filled with a wild hope, I looked around the black marble bathroom. In the huge mirror I saw reflected twelve red roses. They had been carefully arranged in the crystal vase of which Sitt Zulaykha had been so proud. They were perfect.

114

I jumped up and went over to the flower stand. I took out the roses and then returned to the jacuzzi. As I was about to kneel down I happened to look at myself reflected in the other wall mirror. At first, I was startled because I had not noticed the mirror and thought someone had suddenly entered the bathroom without my having heard a thing. I stood up and walked over to the wall, always staring into my own eyes. I had become so strange to myself that I looked at this image with the fascination of someone able to stare at another without being observed. Like a psychiatrist looking through a one-way mirror, or a plaintiff looking over a lineup of suspects in search of the one responsible for the crime, or a veiled woman staring at an American male tourist.

I touched my face, pulled slightly below the eyes, and the stranger did as I did. I withdrew, so did the stranger. I picked up some of the roses I had let slip to the floor. So did the stranger. I turned around in alarm and saw the stranger always in front of me, always mimicking me. I turned around myself. At first slowly. For the first time, I noticed that the walls were mirrors. I started to spin around and I saw a dirty, disheveled old woman clutching a wilting bunch of red roses spin with me. I had to call Maryam.

Maryam
August 5, 1990

Hasan had been Mama's favorite brother. The youngest of the four siblings, Mama had taken special care of him while Sitti was in prison. Although they had had servants and her grandmother had directed the household, there was no one to give little Hasan the love and attention that a three-year-old needs. After Sitti's arrest, Mama was taken out of the convent school and she became responsible for her baby brother. When Sitti was released four years later, she was too tired, too exhausted to fill the shoes that her husband had left empty. The British had broken her. Her two elder brothers had always lived far away. Unlike her, they had not been taken out of school, and in due course they had left for the Americas. So Mama and Hasan had become very close.

Sitti had often spoken of Hasan. She criticized her two other sons for leaving, but she never said a word against Hasan. And here was Hibba, his daughter and the delight of his eye. When he had come to visit just before they went to Kuwait, he had been full of stories about his darling Hibba. She was the prettiest and smartest girl in al-Mansur, the prosperous district in Baghdad where they lived. She was only eight, but his hopes for her were high. He wanted her to go to university, perhaps in Europe, and to be a fabulous success. Sitti told me that the only cloud on this clear horizon was Nuha, Hasan's wife from Sulay-maniya. She did not approve of Hasan's hopes for Hibba. Wasn't she a girl? And shouldn't girls stay at home? Wait to get married? The only thing that really mattered to Nuha was what the neighbors might think. Hasan kept in touch with Sitti and me after they left for Kuwait. Hibba had done well at school, but her mother and the neighbors had had their way: Hibba did not leave the country for university. I had thought of her during the war with Iran. But we heard little from Baghdad during those eight years. I assumed she wasn't married because that kind of news manages to travel. Was she living at home? What had happened to Uncle Hasan's dreams?

"What inspired you to come here?"

"Father spoke of you all the time. Of all of you. And of his dream to return. I knew that he would probably not come back until Aunt Assia returned. He still thinks of her as his mother. In fact, when Sitti died he was less sad than he had been when he heard from you that Layla had let his sister down and that Afaf would not be treated."

Hibba paused and watched me stir the soup.

"He wanted to do something but didn't know how."

"I could never understand why Mama refused to accept help from any of her brothers. The ones in America were one thing, but she loved Uncle Hasan."

"I think I understand. Father used to describe her as proud

and stubborn. He talked about her work building up the child care centers. And when people suggested that this kind of work was women's work, not important, he would explode in anger. He's a real feminist!"

Hibba spoke proudly of him.

"Mother could not stand to hear talk of her. When I grew up, I realized that she must have been terribly jealous of this wonderful woman who could do no wrong."

During the first few days Hibba had kept pretty much to herself, and Arik and I had let her be. Clearly, something had happened, and she needed time and space to recover. She used the room that had once been Afaf's, and in the beginning she spent most of her time there, sleeping and reading.

On the fifth day, she had awakened as though for the first time refreshed.

"Maryam, feel like making a little trip with me?"

"What do you have in mind?"

"I'd love to go to Nablus."

"Why Nablus, of all places? You know, since the Uprising Nablus has been one of the most policed areas. And the roads are quite dangerous. I haven't been there in almost three years."

"Is that a good reason not to go now?" Hibba teased.

I was struck by the change. She had become bright and energetic. In the current atmosphere of gloom, with all the strikes and prohibitions on any kind of celebration, it was suddenly tempting to do something a bit different. Hibba's enthusiasm was contagious.

"Well?" Hibba smiled encouragingly.

"I still don't understand the fascination with Nablus. You

haven't seen a thing in Jerusalem and you're already antsy to leave."

"Oh, I'm not planning to do any sightseeing." Hibba interjected quickly. "There's someone there I'd love to meet."

"Who's that?"

"Sahar Khalifa."

" The writer?" I was curious.

"Exactly."

"But why?"

"I've read everything of hers I could lay my hands on. I really like the way she writes and over the years she has allowed me to keep up, more or less, with what was going on here. It was much better than the newspapers. Much more vivid."

"But she's a novelist. She exaggerates. Did you imagine all of us out there in the streets burning tires?"

"Why not? It fitted Father's scenario."

So we went. I felt guilty going on a jaunt, but what good could I do sitting in the apartment and waiting in vain for news from the Gulf. Things were so tense that it was hard to sit still. Always waiting for something to happen, doing nothing until it did, our helplessness dripping like acid in our veins.

We attached the blue license plates that marked our car as coming from the Occupied Territories and not from inside. They made driving through the hills between Jerusalem and Nablus much easier. We placed the kaffiyeh on the dashboard to show we were with the Intifada. How beautiful and peaceful the countryside looked, yet up above along the crest of the hills the road that the settlers built to connect their places loomed large and threatening. I felt small.

Sahar welcomed us warmly. She and I knew each other slightly, and when I told her that Hibba was a fan, she seemed happy to know that someone, a Palestinian, far away had read her work so carefully and appreciatively. After preparing the coffee and showing us around the apartment she had turned into an office, Sahar invited us to sit in the parlor.

"Many don't like what I write," she told us. "They have their own ideas about what I should write. Take my latest novel. It's not out yet. I've not yet received a printed copy, but I have already received calls from 'outside.' They're telling me that's not the kind of stuff I should be writing. They don't read the whole novel, they just skim looking for passages that may cause problems. They think they're more nationalist than me, but they don't live with the situation day by day."

Sahar paused reflectively. A young man dropped by to leave a bag of prickly pears. It was about the only fruit available at the moment.

"So what's the new novel about?"

Hibba's curiosity had been piqued.

"A freedom fighter falls in love with a prostitute and discovers that she's neither a prostitute nor a collaborator, as everyone claims."

"How does it end?"

Hibba was eager to know the outcome. Did this writer perhaps have a vision for the future? Politicians clearly did not.

"She looks out of the window at the street. There she sees some guys climbing up the wall surrounding the Israeli military compound. But, of course, as they reach the top, they are shot. She can't believe her eyes, wondering if this is some kind of collective suicide. She hears that they are trying to get into the compound to blow it up. She leads them through her kitchen trapdoor into an underground passage that ends up in the middle of the courtyard of the compound. And she throws the Molotov cocktail."

I thought of Sitti and the British. She had been careful when she had talked about the men, always cherishing her martyred husband's memory. But even when I was little I had detected an edge. She had produced faded sepia photographs glued into cloth-covered albums, and she told me what it had been like to march through the streets in a group of women. The men had not stopped them, but then Sitti had always added, they never quite believed in what these women were doing. It was only when their demands had met with some success that the men took them at all seriously.

I had worn out the edges of the photographs as I had gone through them again and again, and tried to imagine that the frail little woman who sat in front of me was the lithe figure in the middle of the image. Head held high, eyes flashing above the white face veil, she was striding out ahead of the rest. A wave of sadness washed over the memory.

I looked out onto the street below. A jeep was passing. After the headiness of the first Intifada successes, the Israelis had resumed control. They were everywhere.

Hibba

August 5, 1990

"I'm back! I couldn't find any mint. But I'll try at the central market after lunch. There should be some then."

Maryam had invited some people for dinner. At first, I thought it was a crazy idea since we were all so tense. But it turned out to be just the right thing to do. A perfect, pretty much mindless thing to do while we waited for the news bulletins.

I laid out the grape leaves, piled small dollops of tomato and rice and herbs in the centers and then rolled and folded the leaves into stubby little cigars, which I then added to other such cigars in the bottom of a large saucepan.

I finished peeling a little pile of garlic cloves and half a dozen onions. Maryam went over to the cupboard and fetched a mortar and pestle.

"Where was I?" I felt a bit foolish having lost my train of the thought.

"You were talking about your trip to Kuwait."

"Oh, yes. When Father came back from Sitti's funeral, he

told me he was going to visit them in Kuwait. He wanted me to come along. Mother couldn't make it. Probably just as well."

"So, did you go? I had no idea that Uncle Hasan had been to see them. Certainly not that you had . . . They never wrote about it . . ."

"That's strange."

"Because it went quite well. Not exactly the great reunion I'd imagined. But it was good finally to put faces to names. Afaf was lovely. We had a good time."

"You did!?"

"Of course we did. Particularly after she showed me some of her paintings."

I was perplexed. Why hadn't they written to Maryam? I remember the trip vividly. I was feeling cooped up with Mother monitoring every move. I was longing for an adventure. I wanted to get away, to see the world. We stayed with Layla. She was welcoming, if never there. Always out at meetings, vernissages, literary gatherings. What a life! I told Maryam about the sense of excitement I'd felt while I was there.

"I had no idea the cultural scene was so active."

I noted an edge of jealousy.

"I doubt that it's always like that," I said quickly. "It was probably the time of the year. November is cooler. That's when the international visitors come."

"Did Layla include them in any of this?" Maryam sounded hesitant.

"Yes, she did." Maryam looked relieved and I knew that she knew about Layla.

"She took us to the fall festival, where we met Iraq's leading woman artist. Later that week, there was an opening reception for her work, and Afaf and I went. She instantly took to Afaf. She devoted herself entirely to her, explaining her canvases to her in detail. Afaf would nod her head in excitement or point to something questioningly. She's so expressive."

What I didn't tell Maryam, decided it would be better not to, was that Layla had not included them in anything else. No, I'm wrong. There was that stiff dinner where we talked about everything but them. Basil was working for an engineer who was distantly connected, and there had been some embarassment. It was quite a relief when they left. Between Basil's coldness, Assia's nervousness, and Afaf's silence, and then Layla's chitchat about Kuwaiti high life, Father and I had not found a comfortable space to speak.

Later, I had spoken to Layla about them and she had shrugged impatiently.

"What more do you want us to do?"

Her attitude toward them made me wonder what she was thinking about us.

"Did they go with you to the reception?" Maryam's voice broke into my reverie.

"Just Uncle Basil. He was amazed at their interaction and he kept asking me about the artist. How were they communicating? Did she know sign language? He wanted to know."

"Tell me about Afaf," Maryam interrupted. She seemed uninterested whenever I mentioned Uncle Basil.

"What did she look like? Can you imagine that I've not seen her for twenty-three years!"

"Well, I've not seen her for ten. But ten years ago, she was lovely. Unusual but lovely."

"What do you mean 'unusual'?" Maryam sounded alarmed.

"Just the hair," I said dismissively, "so short and white."

"Short and white! What did she do with the beautiful long black hair? That's one memory I've cherished. Washing it, mixing the henna, and putting it on her hair, and then mine. We walked around with our hair wrapped in newspaper and plastic bags, laughing at each other. Then I'd wash her hair and then mine and then wait for our hair to dry and to shine red in the sunlight. Hers was so dark it took longer to change color, even to catch henna highlights. How lovely it was next to her translucent porcelain skin! I can't believe she cut it!"

I decided not to tell Maryam about Afaf's clothes. There were so many things about that visit that I felt I had to keep to myself.

I had persuaded Uncle Basil to let me take Afaf to a party that was being thrown in honor of the artist. Reluctantly, he agreed. But then, when he heard how late it was going to start, he changed his mind. Afaf's eyes flashed angrily, and she walked off. There was no way I was going to interfere in a lifetime of habits and then just leave. But as I watched her, I had a vivid sense of what it must be like to live without hope. The future was that place she didn't dare to imagine.

"So did you go to their place?"

I poured the rice out onto the kitchen table and started picking through it, looking for tiny stones.

"It's quite nice. Nicer than I had expected. Five-story buildings with shops on the street and apartments above."

I wasn't just saying that to make Maryam feel better. I remember being relieved to find how pleasant the neighborhood was. Very clean and quite bustling. They were in one of the better buildings.

"Afaf loved her room, which she hung with her own paintings. Flowers and cats mostly. Oils and some watercolors."

Maryam seemed genuinely concerned when she asked whether these were the only paintings Afaf had.

"No, there were some very dark ones but she didn't hang them. She'd done some Intifada paintings—probably working from newspaper photos. But she did hang one I didn't like much. Very dark. It seemed to be a room, a corner of a blackened room and then, when you looked really carefully, you could see two figures sort of collapsed on each other."

"Oh, my God! Don't tell me she's kept it."

"You know it?"

"Well, it might not be the same one. The one she showed me years ago was mostly black, with shades of red and green."

"Sounds like the same one to me. Those were the colors, although the overall general impression was just deeply dark."

"Unless she painted lots of the same scene, that has to be it. It was so violent. Indecent almost."

"Maryam, really!" I couldn't help thinking what a prude she was, how uptight, "It was excellent. Some Goya influence. I think she liked it when I told her. What I couldn't quite understand was that she would want to hang it on her walls with the flowers. But the contrast was striking, and she clearly liked it."

Maryam looked annoyed.

"She's good. She's really good. I wanted to take her back to

Baghdad with me. But your parents seemed against it . . . Your parents, I hope you don't mind my saying so, but they really stifled her."

"Don't imagine you're telling me news!"

" They absolutely refused. Uncle Basil said something about not needing charity, and then Father got angry."

We had both felt bitter and rejected and I realized that we must have thought that in a few days we could change their lives. We never went back but I did keep vaguely in touch with Afaf. We wrote to each other, and usually included some drawing. Over the years, I have felt guilty wondering whether I shouldn't have been more insistent. She was so talented, and where she was no one knew her or knew how to help her.

Afaf
August 6, 1990

Who is this woman? Screaming, whirling, grimacing at herself in the mirror, then returning to stare at me, to prod me. My mother? The woman who needed an answer for every question, a solution to all problems, but who never had the time to think things through. She is transformed, liberated from the weight of the scarf. Her long, gray hair a halo around her wild eyes, a huge crown of soft thorns. I look at her and I feel a surprised, sudden tenderness for this person I have avoided, rejected all my life. Mother. What does that word mean? And for the first time, and from deep inside me, I feel a terrible, painful throb. Mother is the closest thing to me, closer than anything or anyone else can be to me. I must get up, get out of this bath, and go to her and hold her because she needs me. For the first time she needs me. Why can't I move? I can see. I can hear. I can feel the tepid warmth of the water soaking my skin. I can smell the sweetness of the roses scattered on the marble floor. But I cannot move. I have always been alone, always savored my space, kept others out. I let Father in but the more he needed me, the tighter he held me, the further I floated out there where feelings are not touched, where I was safe. The Little Princess on her planet talking to the bushes and the clouds and the foxes. Then, one fine day, I discovered that I had lost my space machine, that the bridges had blown up, and that I was completely, irrev-

ocably alone. And so I painted. I painted closeness and happiness and terror
and a world of friends with whom I could speak. Mother, please come close to
me. Let me tell you a story. It is a story about a girl who thought no one loved
her. She was a good girl and she tried not to bother anyone and to do what she
thought they wanted her to do. It took her a long time to realize that they did not
want her to do anything, to be anything. They wanted her to go away. So she
did. She decided that she would cease to be, by staying absolutely still and the
same. For fourteen years, she wore the same things. In winter, a pair of loose
khaki trousers, a big khaki sweater with a deep cowl neck and the men's shoes her
mother had brought back for her father but which had been too small. They
were brown brogues, very narrow and scarcely worn. They were perfect. In
summer, the girl wore light khakis and a long khaki overshirt, and always the
shoes. Her mother could not understand the obsession with the shoes. But then
there wasn't much about the girl that anyone could understand. Particularly
not after the summer of 1976. That was just before the shoes. The girl was
twenty. It had been a hot, hot day, too hot for long hair. Although the girl loved
her hair and constantly combed it to make it shine, and she loved the fact that
everyone loved it, she was just too hot. So she cut it off. She set up a little mirror
against the window frame and covered the floor around her chair with newspapers. Soon the print disappeared under the puffy piles of long, shining, chocolate brown hair. The mother stopped at the door and then coldly cried: "Why
did you cut off your beautiful hair? What will Baba say? We never cut it.
Twenty years. With those trousers and the hair people won't know you're a
woman." And from her place on that planet, the Princess smiled. She had pulled
up the drawbridge and she knew she was safe. She resumed the cutting as though
her mother were not there. She was absorbed in the task. She would stare in the
mirror and then carefully pick a lock. She combed the strands of hair until they
were perfectly lined up and spilling straight over the palm of her hand. Then,
slowly and precisely, she cut along the edge of her forefinger. When she had cut

the last hair of that strand, she moved on to the next. The woman stood there transfixed. For hours, she watched her turn into a boy. She was helpless. She had arrived too late to do anything about it. Half the mane lay strewn over yesterday's news. When she had finally finished, when the hair was cropped close to her face, the Little Prince smiled at his reflection. He passed his palms over the surface of his head, shuddering with pleasure. He could not get enough of staring at himself. He turned his head this way and that, and the hair did not move. Then, he stood up, pushed the chair back, and wrapped the hair in the paper. He bundled it all up and then left the house in the direction of the desert. The mother did not stop him, not even when he left without veiling his body and what was left of his hair. He knew he was safe. He knew he could paint without fear of betrayal. No longer would he have to lock the box, put the key in his pocket, and keep guard. But the Little Prince did not quite like how he looked. He still looked like her. In the morning, he told his mother he needed some money. She said she was shopping anyway, so what did he want? The Little Prince insisted and the mother relented. When she returned from work, she recoiled from my bleached head. I liked how my olive skin glowed dark against the shimmer of the white hair. My black eyebrows cut slashes above my green eyes. You looked strangely afraid. You nodded absently in my direction and went about the business of preparing dinner, pretending that nothing had happened. But I knew you were afraid. Father, too. And I knew I was safe. And I had held on to it, to my face. I had made it strange so that I alone could look at it, be surprised and delighted by its loveliness, hold it in its thin frame of fine white silk. It was mine. I shared it with no one. Until today. When he came in. He seemed lost as though looking for a place to hide. I sat with this stranger as though with a neighbor, a friend, my friend. My first friend. And then he kissed me. Gently, his lips brushed my black brows, my green eyes. I touched his arm, his shoulder, his neck. I touched the skin of his neck. He was trembling. I felt his fear. I felt his desire.

Hibba

August 6, 1990

We'd been up half the night, alternately drinking coffee and arrack, nibbling on nuts or sucking sweets. The dinner party had gone well. They particularly liked some of the Iraqi dishes that I'd prepared. The guests stayed until two in the morning.

We packed the kibbe into a round tupperware, the tabbouleh into a large square one, and the *fettet dajaj* I scraped into the dog's bowl. It would be no good tomorrow when the pieces of toast would have swollen and absorbed all the chicken broth and yogurt.

Arik went to bed, and Maryam and I stayed up. We weren't tired. There was too much tension, too much uncertainty. And there were news flashes on the hour.

"Coffee?" Maryam seemed anxious to talk. "Come on, you told me you'd tell me about that guy."

I felt myself blush.

"Promise you won't tell anyone. Not even Arik?"

"Cross my heart and hope to die. What was he like?"

"Tall, dark and handsome! What did you expect? Seriously though, it was pretty sick. I keep wondering how I, of all people,

131

could have let myself be drawn into an affair with the notorious Aziz.

"Ever since I was a teenager, I thought I would grow up like all those heroines I'd admired. I'd thought that I was better than my school friends who had quickly married and had children. I saw them proudly produce one baby after the other. Actually, not so proudly when the baby was not a boy. From the moment they clapped eyes on the man of their life, they could only think of their patriotic duty: have lots of boys. Well, as you know, that was not for me. I was going to study for as long as I could, get a job, hold on to my independence. Then in 1985, in the middle of the war, along came Aziz. I was with Nur but in another department. Public Relations. Job description: Take out new clients.

"That night it was Chez Wanisse, the new French-American restaurant where the chic of Baghdad went to be seen. I was there with the boss and a loud American couple . . . What was his name? Bill. Bill White. His wife was one of those ridiculous women who had lived in Lebanon for two years, who knew ten words of incomprehensible Arabic, and who went on and on about the Middle East as though she owned it. They were shouting together when my boss noticed someone walk into the restaurant: 'Aziz!'

"Everyone in the restaurant looked at us. Aziz made his way through the tables to our corner. He chatted with the men for a while. Then, Bill remembered his wife and me. I was wearing a little black dress I had just bought. I loved it, even though it was a bit risqué, big scoop in the back, quite scooped in the front also. Lots of sequins and rhinestones. Not everyone approved, but I didn't care! My boss asked Aziz whether he would join us for dinner, and he did, after getting rid of the two characters with whom he had come. The dinner conversation was utterly civilized after that—not at all the evening I had dreaded. When the evening was over, Aziz insisted on driving everyone home. He dropped me off first and then drove the Americans to their hotel.

"The next morning, I felt wretched. I didn't know what had hit me. After the fling with Peter in Lebanon three years earlier, I'd not been interested in a single man. But even with Peter, I'd not felt like this. I could not get his face out of my head. I kept rehearsing what he had said. I couldn't pull myself together to go to work. So I called up and told the secretary I could not come in, but if anyone called, she could give them my number and they could reach me at home. I had a terrible headache. She must have thought that I'd had too much to drink. The Whites were big potential customers and I was sure everyone would be talking about me. The fridge was empty. As usual. I went out to get some bread and cheese from the corner grocer and when I climbed the stairs to the apartment, there were the roses. A dozen red roses."

Rrrr . . .

"Hello. Is that Ms. Lughod's residence?"

". . ."

"Hello, someone there?"

"Hibba Lughod speaking."

My voice must have sounded funny, a bit choked.

"Good afternoon, this is Aziz Salih. We met last night. I'm the man who drove you home last night."

"Oh, hello."

"I hope you don't mind my calling you at home? I called the office and they told me to call you at home."

"That's fine," I whispered into the receiver.

"I enjoyed meeting you last night, and was wondering whether you might do me the honor of joining me for dinner."

"Well . . ."

"Are you doing anything tonight."

I paused.

"You're doing something else. Never mind. Another time."

"Actually, I'm free."

As soon as the words were out, I felt an idiot. How could I just say yes to a stranger? He must think I was some cheap tramp. The only solution was to be pretty cool and distant throughout the evening.

He picked me up several hours later and was elegant throughout the evening. He asked me about my family, my work. I told him about Afaf. I told him more than I thought I would, because he was so attentive. When he'd asked me what she was like, I had shown him a photograph and he had exclaimed at the similarity. It was the first time it had occurred to me there was any resemblance.

"You could be sisters!"

I told him how much I wanted to bring Afaf to Baghdad. Not then, of course, but after the war . . . God willing there would be an after the war. At the end of the evening, he drove me home, opened the car door, and merely extended his hand and thanked me.

Every night for two weeks, he took me places he thought I might like, including a poetry competition that went on until four in the morning. It was terrific. But before I knew what was happening, I had moved in with him—at least, when he was in town. Candlelit dinners, champagne. Always champagne. An elaborate gift. And then the bad part. He'd tell me stories. He was in the army. I never could quite tell what it was that he did. He was evasive. At first, I was intrigued. Maybe it was too painful to discuss. That was like Peter, and might well be the reason I stuck with him as long as I did. With time, however, what he did elsewhere seemed so remote that it was as though it was happening to someone else. Especially the stories. Fanciful stories that could not all be true, if indeed any of them were.

The final straw came after Al Faw, the island in the Gulf that the Iranians had taken from Saddam. There was a big battle to regain it. The Iraqi Ministry of Culture sent lots of writers and artists there to celebrate it in ink and paint. Everyone was happy, hoping that this triumph would finally mark the end of the war. Aziz had been gone longer than usual.

He called. I came. We talked, drank, ate, made love. Then, when we were comfortable in bed, smoking, he told me a story. That was how it usually worked. But this one was a truly crazy story about a fierce Iranian whom he'd fought off and whom he'd finally executed. It was not so different from most of the stuff I had been listening to for the past three years, but maybe I was finally tired. Sick and tired of Aziz and the medals he had had made in the suq.

"Would you repeat that!?"

"With pleasure! I've tolerated this rubbish year after year. But this is too much!"

He hit me. He hit my face. Once. Twice. He lashed out against my entire body. I had curled up into a small ball tucked into the corner of the bed. He tried to pry the arms away from my head, but I had a firm hold on my elbows. He kept hitting, but I made no sound. He must have thought he was not hurting me. So he went on and on for what seemed like forever.

Then, as suddenly as the madness had taken hold, it dissipated.

An ice cold radiated out from the center of my skull, down my spine, and then split to course down my legs. Exhausted, I slumped down on the bed. I could hear him breathing hard, almost choking.

The seconds ticked by slowly and silently. Carefully, I lowered my arms. I straightened my back so that I was sitting up against the headboard, my breathing so light it might as well not have been. He stretched out a finger to brush a tress that had fallen over my eye.

The touch broke the stunned silence. My composure collapsed and I started to cry. At first, guardedly as though I did not want to disturb anyone or anything. He inched closer. I covered my stinging face with my hands and sobbed. Aziz took me in his arms and rocked me like a baby.

"I'm so sorry, Hibba my darling. Please forgive me. *Hayati inti*, you're my life. The dearest thing in the world to me. I love you, my heart. I love you. My God, what have I done?"

I let him hold me, as the tears flowed ceaselessly and finally uncontrollably. When he made love to me a few moments later, I still did not resist. He was very gentle.

He got out of bed and went to the bathroom.

I didn't move. My face was streaked with welts and the black of the mascara that had run with the tears. My usually perfect hair was disheveled. I did not look good. And for the first time, I did not care. Time passed. I don't know how long.

"Hibba," he said.

I didn't reply. My tongue was heavy.

"Hey! Cat got your tongue. You're not still angry, baby?"

He stroked my hair. I felt nothing.

"How often do I have to tell you that I'm sorry?"

The next morning at nine, I called Nur Agency. The receptionist answered and I told her to give the boss a message. Over the speaker phone came the voice.

"You sure? Why don't you call back at ten and tell him yourself."

"No. Just tell him that I'm resigning and that I'll confirm in writing."

Just as I was replacing the receiver, he burst into the room and shouted.

"What's got into you? You can't resign just like that!"

I said nothing.

"Why did you do that?" he persisted.

"I can't go in looking like this."

He looked at me incredulously.

"You're resigning because you're not looking your best!"

His voice was shrill.

Calmly, I went on.

"I swore on the day after I met you with those Americans, the day I stayed home because I was feeling sick with anxiety and desire for you, that I would never take another instant of sick leave. Especially not because of trouble with a man."

"I see. It's my fault. Now you're going to blame me for making you lose your job. Anyway, you don't look too bad. A bit of makeup and no one would notice."

He looked at me as though trying to be objective.

"You could have said that you had fallen, or bumped into something . . ."

"Or something."

I did not leave the bedroom for five days. I only left the bed for the bathroom. For five days, I left the mascara streaks, as the swellings rose and fell and gradually faded. By the evening of the fifth day the bruising had faded to a sickly yellow with brownish purple spots. He wouldn't leave me alone. Constantly hovering over me and bringing me things to eat and drink. Things I didn't want. I wasn't hungry, I just wanted him to leave me alone. I asked him to go out and buy me some green lipstick. I'd read somewhere that green lipstick is good to cover blemishes.

"A handy tip for the busy, battered wife!"

He was less amused than I was. But he went. My only regret is that I was not there to see his face when he found me gone.

I had forgotten Maryam and suddenly realized that she was staring at me. I had no idea how long I had sat there, sunk in a reverie. I was grateful to her, glad she had not asked me to tell her my thoughts.

"Did he ever call you after the roses?" Maryam was tentative.

"Yes, that afternoon, and pretty soon I was in deep in something that finally became too hard to control. That was why I had to get out. Aziz, in a funny way, was the reason that I decided to come here."

Aziz

August 1, 1990

"May God give you success. May you be instrumental in reat-
taching our dear Kuwait to its kinsfolk in Najaf, in Baghdad, in
Kirkuk, in Nineveh, and here in Karbala."

My father-in-law raised his hand to shoulder-level, palm
facing out toward me and the dignitaries gathered around the
perimeter of the *majlis.* There was polite applause as those present recognized Saddam's words.

I stood in the middle of the room. I could see myself, tall
and handsome in the uniform. My glistening black hair was
slicked into place, the V-shaped mustache perfectly trimmed to
cut off at the corners of the mouth. I placed my right hand flat
on my chest just above my heart and bowed slightly. A gesture I
felt to be full of pride and grace.

I was preparing for the last act. This time, I would not
return.

"I'll show that bitch I'm not the beast she thinks I am. I'll get
them out of there. I'll bring them to her in Baghdad. I'll show her!

She'll be sorry she just walked off like that. This time she'll have to believe me because it will be true."

Hibba told me that they lived not far from the Palestinian embassy in Hawalli. That shouldn't be too hard to find.

But here and now, the farewell should be noble and impressive.

Al Capone. Jimmy Stewart. Humphrey Bogart. They all flashed before my eyes.

The dignified silence of the *majlis* was interrupted by the sound of sniffling. Someone was crying. Sanaa. Of course! Exceptionally, Sanaa had joined the men. As the wife of the hero-to-be, she was allowed to break protocol for this special occasion.

I glanced quickly in her direction. I had to get away.

What if it's not so easy to find them? I might be killed . . .

Oh, my God. I felt slight panic. I looked at the old man who had noticed the moment. The watery, gray eyes of the turbaned old man hardened, darkened. Two black beads burrowed into my soul.

This was not Sanaa's father.

It was the old man in the hut.

No, it's father. Father's back.

Even at this moment, when he should be the proudest of his son, he haunts and mocks me.

My breathing quickens. The siren sounds, announcing the roll call. I feel the color drain out of my face. I feel giddy, light-headed. Will I never be rid of those eyes? The black beads strip away the veneer and I'm back in the hut with that helpless old man, fighting the hallucinations.

"Never fall on your knees. Never let them shoot you in the back. Never soften. Never buckle under. Never waiver. Never . . . Never . . . Nev—"

A little later and as though out of a fog, I hear voices.

"Call a doctor! He may have had a heart attack."

People jump up out of their chairs and the room's in an uproar. By the time the doctor arrives, I am fine. No, it's not a heart attack. She insists that the doctor check again, more carefully.

"Aziz couldn't have fainted without good cause."

The doctor checks again and then comes up with the same verdict.

"Your husband is fine. Maybe it's the heat?"

"But it's not particularly hot."

"Well, I don't know . . . It's probably the stress of going off to battle."

"That will do, Doctor," I interrupt.

"At all events," the doctor resumes as though he had not heard, "he needs some rest."

"Do stop fussing, Sanaa."

I pull myself together and stand there brushing off my no-longer-quite-so-crisp uniform.

"Don't be ridiculous! I don't have time to rest. My unit is leaving in an hour and I have to pack. Get me some water."

Maryam

August 6, 1990

The outing to Nablus had been a great success. We'd stayed for
tea and fruits and then had left just before dark. We talked all the
way home about our hopes and plans, and about Afaf. The next
two days had been quiet and nerve-racking. Still no word from
them. No word about them. Just CNN reports about the dire
conditions. The burning, looting, and raping. Mostly, we
avoided the subject. There was nothing new to say. A strange
boredom was in the air.

"Where's the olive oil?" Hibba was making an upside-down
chicken dish.

"Isn't it up to your right?"

"No."

I stopped chopping the onions and after looking in all the
usual places, I went out onto the kitchen balcony.

"Here it is."

"What's the time?"

"11:52."

"Almost time for the noon news."

I pulled out of the desk drawer the little shortwave radio Baba had given me for my sixteenth birthday, The BBC news reported that the Iraqis were deep into Kuwait City. Baghdad radio was once again broadcasting Saddam Hussein's "Victory Day" message: "At a time when the second of August arrived to be the legitimate newborn son of the second Qadisiya and its people—and with God's help, it will also be a loyal son—it and its consequences will be the beginning of a new, lofty, and rising stage in which virtue will spread throughout the Arab homeland in the coming days and profanity, treachery, betrayal, meanness, and subservience to the foreigner will retreat from it . . ."

The delicious aroma of onions in olive oil filled the apartment, and I opened the kitchen door to let out the steaminess.

"What took place on 2 August was inevitable so that death might not prevail over life . . ."

Then our attention was caught by the following words.

"The lowly wanted and planned to harm the free women of Iraq, as they had done to free Arab women in other places. But their calculations went wrong because they did not know that we prefer death to this and that we cannot sleep without putting out the eyes of those who encroach upon Iraqi and Arab and Islamic values."

Hibba was shaking her head in disbelief.

"The hypocrite! As long as we have men like him pretending to protect our honor, we may as well just gird up our loins and offer our bodies to the first customer who comes along."

I interrupted Hibba's tirade impatiently.

"Oh, do stop it. I'm glad he's done what he's done, glad he's screwed those pimps."

"You know who's the biggest pimp of all?"

I raised my right eyebrow skeptically awaiting another out-
burst, knowing that whatever I said would not stop it.

Hibba told me some unbelievable story, more a rumor that
had begun to spread after the end of the war, about the special
unit whose special assignment it was to "violate women's honor."

"Don't be ridiculous, Hibba. How could you be so naïve as
to believe such nonsense?"

Hibba smiled. She got up and put her arms around my
sweaty neck. A faint whiff of Chanel.

"That was how I reacted when I first heard about it. It's how
any rational person would and should react. But we're not deal-
ing with a rational person. He's crazy, power-crazy, and he
knows that his most dangerous enemy is his own people, once
they wake up to their own power. This time he may just have
gone too far. It's the women he's claiming to protect who may be
his most dangerous enemy. We were told to have five children,
preferably boys, for the country and its struggle. As an unmar-
ried professional woman, I could not morally do my moral duty.
Some zealous patriots urged me to marry, marry anyone, if nec-
essary don't marry, but 'Please, ya Hibba, you must have babies.
At least one!' And then I would ask, 'What if it's a girl?' Just to test
their reactions."

Hibba chuckled as she thought back on those surreal en-
counters.

The doorbell rang.

Hibba opened the door. It was Nadia, the young woman
from downstairs.

"What is it?" I called from the living room.

"It's Nadia. She says there's a call for you."

It had to be them.

"Who is it? Are they still on the line?"

Nadia shouted that, no, they were not.

"Nadia, come in. Who was it?"

"It was your mother."

I was both alarmed and relieved. Four days without any news. I could not wait to speak with her.

"She said that she'd been trying to get through to you but that she could only get a busy signal. So she decided to try me."

Mama was calling. I prayed to God that the news be good. I went over to the telephone that had been unusually quiet all morning. I picked up the receiver. True enough, it was off the hook. Nadia was fidgeting and I was suddenly anxious.

"What's wrong? *Fi shi?*"

My heart was pounding. I had been so absorbed in Hibba's stories that I had briefly forgotten Kuwait.

"Nadia, what did she say?"

"I couldn't hear very well but she sounded a bit . . ." Nadia's voice trailed off.

"My God, you're scaring me. She must have said something?"

"No, she didn't, other than that she would be calling back in a few minutes. You'd better hurry down to my place."

I dropped what I was doing and rushed out of the apartment and down the stairs after Nadia.

"Maryam, *habibti,* is that you? Thank God for that. I've been trying and trying."

"Mama, tell me how you are. Where are you? Where are you

calling from? How's Baba? And Afaf? Has anyone been hurt? I've been worried sick. How . . ."

My questions came out like a shower of bullets, each one tripping over the other in my urgency to know.

"I'm all right. But it's Afaf . . ."

"What's wrong?" The line was crackling and I was afraid of losing the connection. "Is she hurt?"

Silence. The expensive minutes ticked by as I tried to imagine what was going through her head.

"Hayati, are you there?"

"Yes, yes. What's going on? Where are you?"

Silence.

Something had happened. Something terrible.

"Maryam, *hayati,* I love you."

Her voice sounded lifeless, all that I had recognized were the wonderfully warm terms of endearment. *Habibti, hayati.* How long had it been since I had last heard her call me my darling, my life? How many centuries had it been since I had seen those words form on her full lips? But even this pleasure at hearing these words could not overcome my anxiety.

"Mama, please tell me! What's happened to Afaf?"

"They're all right."

But she had just said that something had happened. Then, almost as an afterthought, "They're going to be all right. I'm trying to work things out and I should be with you before long."

"Mama!" I felt again the ache of longing that the years had dulled. I had become a little girl again. The little girl who had always wanted her mother to hold her whenever things went wrong.

"Mama, tell me what's wrong." My voice pierced the line.

"Maryam, if I'm not with you by the end of September, call Layla."

"Mama, be careful. Is there anything I can do?"

"Pray for us."

I heard the click of the phone. Pray! She had actually asked me to pray. And she had not even said good-bye. Over the past twenty-three years, we had spoken so rarely, yet each time we had been at once so intimate, so close I could have reached out and touched her.

"Maryam, what's the news?" Arik came down when he heard the commotion, and he had watched the conversation from the door.

"I hope all's well?" Nadia had chimed in.

"I don't know. I really don't know. But thanks anyway."

I started to walk out.

"Thanks, Nadia, for letting us use your phone. Let's all pray for our friends and families in Kuwait."

Nadia's brother, an engineer, had gone there six months earlier.

Arik stood at the entrance, unsure what to do. As I passed him almost without noticing him, he stretched out his arm and held me.

"How did your Mom sound?"

"Terrible. She sounded very afraid. Arik, can you believe that she asked me to pray?! First, she said something was up with Afaf, and then she said that they were all right and then that she was arranging for them to come back to Jerusalem. Actually, she did not say we. She said I. I should be with you before long. She sounded utterly confused."

In fact, she had not sounded at all like herself.

"That's great! Don't fret. Why, it's exactly what you've wanted for so long!"

We had come to the top of the stairs and I was completely out of breath.

"Hibba," Arik announced, a shade too loud. "Good news! Assia's coming back. She's bringing Basil and Afaf home finally."

As I crossed the threshold, I looked at my uncle's daughter. A real Lughod face. In one of the few photos that Mama had sent years ago, Afaf had been standing in a doorway looking out into the sun. The doorway had framed her so that you could not see what was behind her. Her long chocolate hair fell gracefully around her face and her blank eyes stared straight into the camera. I had been struck by how little my sister had changed. She still looked like a little girl. Although Mama had continued to write regularly once a month, she never sent any more photos. The image I retained was of that lovely, wistful, absent girl.

Afaf

August 6, 1990

"Mother, are you all right? What's wrong with you? Why did you kill him? Wake up. I'm better. Mummy, please! Don't leave me. Say something."

The words came from a place I did not know existed within me. I had spoken. I wanted her to hear me.

I was speaking and I wanted her to hear me and to tell me why she had done it.

Why had she rushed at him with the knife?

I wanted to tell her how it had happened.

There had been a knock at the door and I had opened it. A tall man in uniform.

I immediately recognized the Iraqi uniform. I backed away. Why had he come here? Did he want to harm me? Was he going to kill me? I tried to close the door but he held it. Not violently, just firmly.

"No, please, Ms. Lughod, don't be afraid."

I was paralyzed.

How did this stranger know my name? I felt as though I was

about to have one of my spells. He stood there by the door, just looking at me for the longest time.

"You are Ms. Lughod, aren't you? Afaf Lughod?"

I nodded and raised my hands in astonishment. He seemed amazed.

"You are the spitting image of your cousin."

He started to fumble around in the inner pocket of his uniform jacket. For a second I wondered whether he would, after all, take out a gun and shoot me.

"I am so glad I found you. I've been looking everywhere! This is quite a maze."

He handed me a photograph. Hibba had taken it when she was visiting us in 1977. So, he must know Hibba. How would he have the photo otherwise? I had liked the image at the time. So far from what I am now and I had insisted that mother send it back to Maryam. She had sent it but she had never mentioned the visit nor who had taken the picture. I stepped back into the room and he followed me.

"Oh, I'm sorry, let me introduce myself. I'm Aziz Salih, a friend of Hibba's. She asked me to make sure you were all right. I think we'd better get out of here. It's not safe. We don't have much time. Where are your parents? When do they come back?"

I pointed to my watch.

"Four? So we have about half an hour. Can you start packing? We can only take what can be easily carried."

I piled some things on my bed, and I felt him watch me. Respectful but intense. I got a bit nervous. My heart was beating uncomfortably. I was about to have an attack. I could feel it coming.

"Can I help?"

I shook my head, but sat on the bed to catch my breath. He stood where he was.

"Do you mind if I drink something? I'm so thirsty. My God, it's hot!"

I got up, went over to the refrigerator, and poured a glass of ice water. I added a drop of orange flower essence. He took the glass and our fingers touched. I didn't move. For what seemed like an eternity, we stood there looking at each other. I held his hand and brought him close and I looked in his eyes and saw mine. I looked for the fear but found none. Minutes passed like prisoners dragging stones. I sat with this stranger as though with a neighbor, a friend, my friend. Then he kissed me. Gently, his lips brushed my brows, my eyes. I touched his arm, his shoulder, his neck. I touched the skin of his neck. He was trembling.

The key turned in the lock. The door opened. A bit. Then some more. The calm exploded and then everything went black.

"Mummy, where have you been? I've got to talk to you."

She was back in the bathroom after speaking with someone on the phone, I had heard her shouting as though the line were bad. Although she was still unsteady on her feet, and lurching around, she had stopped the terrible spinning. When she looked in my direction, she clearly saw nothing. Suddenly, she crumpled in on herself. Her wild, gray hair and her torn, wet clothes filled me with tenderness. She still had two of the roses clutched in her right hand. There was a smell of smoke.

"Mummy, say something!"

I felt a sudden surge of strength return and I dragged myself out of the water. My skin was white and wrinkled from soaking.

I wrapped a thick pink towel around my naked body, and then knelt down on the black marble by my mother. I touched her face, stroked her hair. She did not move from the spot where she had finally fallen. I sat down next to her, cross-legged on the floor, and took her head in my lap. Gently, I pulled my fingers through the matted gray locks, gradually freeing her face. She seemed to be asleep. Suddenly, there was a sound of cracking. Then a bang. Not a gun but something collapsing.

"Mummy, can you hear me?"

Unused to touching her, I did not know what to do, where to feel to make sure that she was all right. Where was her heart? The skin was damp and warm. She must be alive.

I shook her gently at first, but then with increasing vigor.

"Mummy, you must wake up! We've got to get out of here. The palace is on fire!"

I felt her move. Her eyes opened slightly. Then popped wide open.

"Afaf?"

There was fear, incredulity but also something else in her voice.

"Yes, Mummy. We've got to go. Here, hold on to me."

Suddenly and for the first time in my life, I was in charge.